Maggie of Long Hollow

James W. Prothero

PublishAmerica
Baltimore

First printing

ISBN: 1-60672-900-4
PUBLISHED BY PUBLISHAMERICA, LLLP
www.publishamerica.com
Baltimore

Printed in the United States of America

To Jane Bruckler and Trish Davenport, who never stopped believing.

I

War Comes to Me

In the fall of my thirteenth year, I first resolved in my heart two things, both treasonous to my father: I was going to marry a man with book learning, and I was going to marry a man who wasn't a Friend. I don't think the war touched me till then. Sure, for near two years, from time to time men in blue and men in grey with big mud-caked boots stopped at our farm in Long Hollow and demanded crops, animals, and even borrowed Father's gun, before they rode off to Cumberland Gap. Once the Yankees bought all of Father's horses except our nag, "Old Pet." The year before some shots were fired down in Jonesville, but all that was ancient history now, long since chewed thin by the old men down at the Jonesville Hotel bar. Still, we'd just got word that General Longstreet had laid siege to the Yankees just down the road at Knoxville. And the war, and my resolve, came to me that Sixth Day afternoon Caleb Pennington pointed out to me what me and my family really were.

"'Bolitionists! Yankee-lovers! Traitors!" Caleb, a dirty, little blond boy, sputtered the words so I could feel them bite me. I lowered my eyes and kept walking, gripping my book strap so hard my nails cut into the leather. The sides of my bonnet framed the muddy road ahead of me and screened out the hateful glare I'd seen on Caleb Pennington's face. A mud clod flew past me.

"Maggie," little William cried, gripping my hand tighter. "He's throwing things at us." William was only seven and smaller than Caleb by far. It was up to me to get us out of this.

"Hush, William. Walk faster. Father says we got to turn the other cheek." Just as the words escaped my lips a great clod exploded in the middle of my back. Tears started around the corners of my eyes, though I tried to stop them. "Just keep walking," I ordered William and tried to quicken my pace. Another clod exploded on the back of my head and sent my bonnet flying. My hair came undone and tumbled over my shoulders. Something angry and warlike gripped my heart. I stopped, turned and fixed on Caleb.

"Thee is a dirty scoundrel, Caleb Pennington and a coward as well to throw dirt at a girl!" That stopped his arm almost in mid throw. I couldn't tell if I'd touched his sense of shame or he was just surprised by my standing up to him. Then he smiled an evil smile and flung the mud clod anyway. William and I stepped aside; the clod rolled harmlessly by my feet. For an instant I thought of my father's cautions. It was too much for me. In my fury I picked up the clod and sent it flying back with all the hatred and strength in my body. Imagine my surprise when it exploded right on Caleb Pennington's nose with a sound like "fop." I laughed without meaning to. Caleb yelped and reached for more dirt. As the mud clods burst on me, my father's words about violence leading to more violence seemed bitterly true.

"Stop that, Caleb Pennington!" a voice interrupted. "You so brave you got to fight girls instead of Yankees?" The voice belonged to Josiah Clark, a tall, dark haired boy two years older than me, the oldest boy at our school and certainly the handsomest. Caleb froze at once. No boy could whip Josiah Clark and Caleb didn't seem ready to try. "Go on," Josiah said, "Get yourself home. Thought I saw Yankees down to your farm." Caleb looked stricken and dashed down the road with his arms flailing like windmills.

I felt like saying a hundred things to Josiah, but I couldn't find the breath to say one. I couldn't even lift my eyes. My heart beat so fast I'm sure they heard it over in Jonesville, seven miles east. He picked up my bonnet and brushed it off, handing it to me. I dared to look up into his face and saw a slight laugh there; not a mean laugh, but as if he thought my shyness funny and didn't mind. My tongue came unglued.

"I thank thee, Josiah."

"Can I walk you home, Maggie?"

I felt my face burn. What would Mama and Father say? Josiah was no Friend and I so young. Josiah produced an apple out of his pocket and chomped a first, dripping bite out of it, holding it toward me as natural as could be.

"No, I thank thee," I said, then realizing I might have answered both questions without meaning to, "But thee can walk William and me home." I took William's hand while he squinted up at me from under the locks of brown hair in his face as if to ask if this was really a good idea. My folk don't mix much with the folk hereabouts and that thought made me angry. We began walking down the avenue of bare branched oaks, a copper colored squirrel scolding us from his hole.

"Mighty fine day, don't you think, Maggie?" Josiah asked. And it was. The chill wind off the bare ridge of Cumberland Mountain to the northwest was scented with the pine forest at its foot. Corn stood in tipi-like shucks in the fields on either side of the road, set off by split rail fences, and pumpkins squatted beneath the shucks. Oh, such a beautiful fall. My heart ached for something, I wasn't sure what. Maybe it lay far beyond Cumberland Mountain, maybe in Josiah's words. But I was knotted up inside just waiting for Josiah to ask me or say something about my folk's strange ways, some word that would cut me like a knife quicker than any spite from Caleb Pennington or any of the other children at our school. Just to hear him say that awful name, "Quaker", would bring me misery for years to come, I just knew.

"Yes, mighty fine," I answered, flustered. Josiah seemed to look far away, over the ridge.

"You know," he said to the distance as much as to me, "my pa and brother James are out there somewheres with Gen'l Lee. I'll be sixteen next summer and I'm goin' out to join 'em, fight for my country." His eyes glowed with pleasure at the thought. I dreaded the next word. Would he bring up the fact that my folk thought war a sin, and refused to lift a gun against any man? I waited for his words to cut me. But he took his eyes off the distance and looked me straight in my eyes. "Would you think of me, when I'm gone, out on the field of battle? Would you, Maggie?"

I didn't know whether to look back into his eyes or study the dust on the road. I knew he wouldn't look away until he had his answer. For Josiah Clark, shyness was an silly thing that other people did; Josiah didn't have a shy bone in his body. Would I think of him then? Didn't I think of him now, day and night? The most charming boy in Lee County?

"Surely, Josiah, I will think of thee."

He brightened up like I had said something important. "Thank you, Maggie, 'cause I know I'll be thinking of you."

My face burned but my heart near leaped out of my breast.

"Maggie! Maggie Milbourn! William Milbourn! Is that thee lollygagging out on the road? Thee should've been home near ten minutes ago." It was Mama's voice, sure. I could see her kneeling in the potato patch by the house. William tugged at my hand. "I must go," I found the courage to say, "But I thank thee, Josiah." William broke into a run and I followed, eager to get away before I said something stupid that I'd regret later.

"'Bout time thee got home," Mama scolded gently. "I'll need thy help digging these potatoes. And thy father will want thee to bring in the cows from the north pasture. William, go give thy father a hand with the pumpkins." She dug vigorously with her spade, popping out the gritty, earth dressed potatoes into her basket. I picked up another spade hard by and did likewise. Next to her, by the side of the house, little Mary and Robert dug mud pies, and baby John slept peacefully wrapped in blankets in a big wicker basket.

"Who was that boy with thee and William?" Mama asked, not looking at me. But I could tell she was burning to know and didn't want to let on.

"Oh," I tried to say as casually as I could, "Josiah Clark. He chased off the Pennington boy and walked us home." I made sure to say 'us' and not 'me', and to play down Josiah's part. Mama stopped her digging and looked up into my face.

"What happened with the Pennington boy?"

"He threw mud at William and me, called us names." I was careful not to mention that I threw some mud back.

She looked over my mud-spattered dress and shook her head. "What sort of names?"

"'Abolitionist,' 'Yankee-lover', and 'traitor.'"

Mama wiped the hair from her face with the back of her hand. Sorrow filled her eyes.

I pressed this moment of silence, "Is it true, Mama?"

"What?"

"Are we all those things?"

"Lord, child, thee don't ask easy questions. Well, we don't believe in slavery. But I don't know if we're as fiery as the abolitionists. Thy father gave Bert and Leah and their children their freedom, don't thee remember?"

I did just remember Leah's ample and warm embraces smelling of calico and molasses, and Bert's storytelling. In my mind I could still see them shake father's hand and hug my mother before they headed north to make a new life for themselves where no one would mistake them for slaves by the color of their skins.

"And we love all men, including Yankees and our enemies too."

I noticed she didn't include Yankees as enemies. So that much must be true.

"And as for being traitors, well, thy father never did care much for leaving the Union, but we lift our hand up against no man." I took this to mean we were traitors too, even if we didn't fight. It seemed to me that not to help someone was to hinder them. Josiah's fathers and brothers were fighting for their country. Mine was running his farm and his mill and going to First Day meetings and bad mouthing his new nation. Caleb Pennington was right; we were guilty on all three charges. The angry, warlike thing grew up in my heart. Right then and there I made my terrible resolve never to marry a 'Quaker', as they called us.

If I was quick to judge my father it was because he was always a severe, placid man. To hear him talk, his love for his fellow man was as warm and wide as a summer field, but my corner of it seemed only to catch the chilly November winds. When I heard the wagon coming around the barn, I straightened up like a soldier does when his officer comes by. William rode up with Father on the seat of the old buckboard pulled sluggishly by Old Pet. Before the war Father had a smart pulling horse in the big bay mare, Ginger. But bushwhackers stole Ginger and some other horses one night back in '62. Nobody ever wanted to steal Old Pet, and in that lay her value. Father's face showed no feelings, be he angry or happy, and that made me angry. I always felt like I had to guess where I stood with him until he spoke, which relieved me some.

"Got to get the last of the corn shucked and into the cribs this week. Better figure a place to hide most of it. Bushwhackers will look in the cribs first."

Mama nodded at the wisdom of this. Father looked at me and frowned a little. "Why is thee so dirty, Maggie? Surely, digging potatoes ain't that hard."

I instinctively lowered my eyes. I didn't want to tell him. Mama spoke up in my behalf. "The Pennington boy was throwing mud at Maggie and William, calling them names."

Father nodded grimly. I half expected to hear the lecture on turning the other cheek again, the one I had ignored that afternoon so disastrously, but instead he said, “Did thee hear the firing last night, Mary?”

She shook her head, ‘no.’ I looked up into his face. My father generally called Mama by her first name when he was troubled; and little ever seemed to trouble him. Even now, his face revealed no emotion. “Seemed like it came from Mulberry Gap. Mighty close, by the sound of it. Less than five miles maybe. Just on the other side of Wallen Ridge. Got a bad feeling, Mary, that the war’s coming closer. Things are going to get rough for thee and the children. Sometimes I wish…”

“No, Henry. Don’t say it. Thee couldn’t have left this country any more than I, nor could thee leave thy father and mother and family. This war can’t last forever.” And she looked far away, up the flame colored hillside where the last of the fall leaves fluttered off the bare branched trees.

Father interrupted the silence with a remark to me. “Go bring the cows in, Maggie. Looks like we better keep ‘em down close to the barn from now on.”

I gladly took this chance to get free of his presence and skipped up the lane, picking a switch off a low maple tree along the way. As I considered father’s words about the fighting at Mulberry Gap, I suddenly recalled waking last night and getting up on my elbows to listen to the odd sound, like slaves beating drums in the hills that had invaded my half waking dreams. So that’s what war sounded like. Last year when the Yankees fought at Jonesville, I’d been too far away to hear the guns. Now I’d heard it, it didn’t sound like I figured it would.

I was thinking these things when I got to our north pasture gate. I was singing to myself too, another thing that Friends weren’t supposed to do as singing got in the way of the Inner Light. But I found that singing songs I learned at school from Miss Emily lightened my heart a little and made my jobs easier. This job should have been as easy as opening the gate and walking the cows back to the barn. The cows generally were happy to go, knowing Mama would relieve their swollen udders. Usually, they waited for me with their big brown inquisitive faces peering over the rail gate. To my dismay, I could see the cows had scattered up into the thick laurel and witch hobble up the side of Cedar Hill. Lord, when the Almighty handed out stupidity, I thought He must have given cows twice the dose. I stomped my foot to relieve my feelings and began climbing over the fence, dress, petticoat, and all. I was just coming down the other side when I heard a horse coming up the lane at full speed, hooves drumming heavy and fast. No one ever rode horses that hard except soldiers when they fought. My body tingled all over and I froze, listening. It sounded like one horse. No. There were more behind, coming up in the distance. I climbed down the rest of the way off the fence and looked around for bushes nearby. I had to get out of sight. But all the cover was twenty or thirty yards from the fence where the cows had eaten it back. I froze; that was better than being caught running.

When I looked up the lane again, I could make out the first rider. He was leaned down low over the neck of his black mount, whose rippling muscles scattered sweat and lather. The black horse plunged on with all its force and the rider kicked it to encourage it more. For a moment I felt greatly sorry for the horse; then I remembered who it belonged to and knew the rider. Tom Bush was my Uncle George's hired man and a Friend. He'd always been mighty kind to me. To think that the conscriptors were out to drag Tom Bush into the army. Tom's horse drew near and right then he saw me and veered toward the gate. My word, he was going to charge the gate!

"Let the bars down, Maggie!" Tom yelled.

I panicked for a second. One is supposed to take the bottom bars off a rail gate first and take the top rail off last. But Tom Bush was coming on like a locomotive, his black mare breathing in short bursts and lathered with perspiration. I didn't think; I just shoved the top rail off as quick as I could. It hit the ground with a hollow, rattling ring and the black horse sailed over the remaining rails like an eagle rising up into the sky. She landed with a heavy clap on my side of the pasture and dashed on without a break in the rhythm of her hoofbeats.

"They're after me, Maggie! Don't tell 'em which way I went!"

And he thundered into the cedar thickets on the far side of the pasture. I didn't hardly have time to breathe before three horsemen rode up to the gate and leaped over it. They loped into the pasture a ways and reined up to a stop. Oh, no, don't let them question me. Oh, Jesus, have mercy and don't let them question me.

I felt too frightened to move or I would have run away, sure. One of them took off his grey slouch hat and made as if to throw it on the ground. I looked at him. He was a big man in a grey wool uniform with riding boots that came up his thigh and insignia on his collar. His thick brown beard and long hair hung down his shoulders. When his horse turned I clearly saw the pistol on his left hip and the saber hanging in a scabbard below it. He looked at me and my throat got very tight and dry. The other two men around him turned their horses too and I got as good a look at them as they did at me. One was tall in the saddle, clean shaven and skinny. He wore butternut brown cotton shirt and breeches, common clothes any farmer might wear, but he wore a grey kepi and carried a small rifle, resting the stock on his thigh and pointing the barrel up. The other fellow dressed much the same and carried another such rifle, but he had a beard. Both carried sabers and pistols like the man in grey.

The man in grey walked his horse up to me and my stomach churned so that I felt sure I'd throw up. I couldn't stop myself from trembling. The man must have noticed it, for he said, "Don't be frightened, little girl. We ain't gonna harm you. We ain't bushwhackers. I'm Captain Garson, 64th Virginia Cavalry." Here he touched the brim of his hat like a gentleman. "We ain't here to steal nothing, just to enlist men under the law. Now tell me," he went on, leaning on the pommel of his saddle to get his face down closer to mine, "You seen which way that feller gone?"

My throat was so constricted I couldn't begin to speak, but I pointed to the cedars across the pasture.

"Yeah, we seen that. But there's a lot of trails up that hill. You reckon you might know which one he took?"

I shook my head no, letting a breath of relief out. I knew I could tell the truth there; I had no idea which way Tom Bush took through that maze of trees and brush. He frowned and I thought he'd kill me sure. The clean shaven rider interrupted.

"Must be a dozen trails up that hillside, Captain. Reckon I wouldn't know which one to take neither."

The Captain didn't seem satisfied with this. "What are you doing here, young lady?"

I swallowed hard and found my voice. "I'm to fetch the cows home."

"Cows? You still got more'n one cow? I see. Your daddy farm around here?"

What could I do? It was a sin to lie. I nodded yes.

"Well, Sergeant, looks like you were right. This county can support the regiment. These people are still fat and some of 'em Quakers to boot. And I'm gonna hunt down every fat, duty-dodging Quaker if it takes me a year."

"Yessir," the Sergeant answered him.

"Very well. Let's move out. Young lady, you think you can take the rest of the rails off for us?"

I rushed to the gate and took off the rest of the rails properly, from the bottom up. The soldiers rode through and the Captain turned, touching the brim of his hat.

"Much obliged, ma'am."

My words came out without a thought, out of trained habit, "Thee is welcome." I clapped my hand over my mouth in horror, but it was too late. Oh please merciful Jesus don't let him hear my foolishness. But as the horses walked away the Captain stared at me intensely. He'd heard! Oh Jesus no! The Captain finally turned around the other way and they walked their horses off down the lane. The moment they were out of sight I forgot the gate and the cows and fled across the lane and down to my secret way home over Mr. Crabtree's fields.

II
I Become a Traitor

When I told father, out of breath, everything that had happened, he looked more grim than usual. Then he looked up to Mama and said, "I'm going after the cows."

"Henry, no. The conscriptors must not see thee."

"I'll be watching for them. I'll take the cows across Bush's place. I need to warn John and Minerva anyways, especially if Tom hasn't made it back and they're worried. And brother George must know. No one will see me except when I cross the road, and then I'll be extra careful."

"Henry. Thee isn't making sense. Maggie is safer."

"Maggie's got the more dangerous job to do. Daughter, thee must take Old Pet and ride into town to Grandfather's house. Go quickly, but don't look like thee is hurrying. Thee must tell Grandfather Andrew and Grandma Mitchie what happened. Tell them they've got to get Uncle Joel out of sight quick as they can. Stay the night there and return tomorrow."

"Henry..." Mama began to plead.

"No, Mary," Father said sternly, "Maggie is the safest. No one will think a thing about Maggie taking Old Pet down to Grandfather's on a Sixth Day afternoon, for it is common."

I didn't wait for Mama to object more. I got out of the kitchen and out to the barn where Old Pet waited in amongst all the empty stalls. The saddle was heavy and Old Pet's back a good sixteen hands high, but she was so slow and spiritless, and her back so flat, that all I needed to put on her was the bridle and reins. When I'd gotten those on, I led her next to the big crate and left her standing while I climbed up and got on. Most horses would have taken that chance to head back to the stall or out the barn door. Old Pet just stood and blew out his nostrils. I jumped up on his back on my belly and swung my leg over the way boys do. I never let mother see me do it; she wouldn't like it much.

"C'mon, Old Pet. Let's head down to Grandfather's."

Old Pet shuffled into a slow, steady rocking motion out the barn and down the lane. It was a journey we usually made on Seventh Day morning, but we'd done it on Sixth Day evening before, most often in the summer. I hardly had to touch the reins or kick him; he knew what I wanted and knew the way, so there wasn't much for me to do with more than an hour and seven miles east of country road to Jonesville ahead of me.

Soon, I got to thinking about all sorts of things. I burned with shame at my slip of the tongue saying 'thee' to the Confederate captain. Surely, if I weren't to make that mistake again, I'd have to learn to talk like the other folk around here. I remembered my resolve not to marry another Friend, and figured it was high time I learned to talk like most folks. "Well, first thing Maggie," I said out loud to myself, "Thee has…you have got to stop saying 'thee' and 'thy.' And…you have got to start calling the days by the names most folks use. Today is Friday, and tomorrow is Saturday."

I thrilled at the use of such wicked language. I often liked talking to myself out loud when I was alone. It seemed a good way to get some thinking done clear and proper like. But having said it out loud, it just didn't seem to want to come naturally. I'd have to think about it when I was around folks. And wouldn't some of them notice the change? When you growed up in Lee County, there weren't no secrets from nobody.

The sun was crawling down the sky to Cumberland Mountain, casting longer shadows on the trees and for a moment the joy of it drowned out the fears in my heart. It was glorious. When I looked up I found I was passing the Clark farm on the left. There weren't much to see up here on the road; the house and the best fields were back in a ways. But just the thought of Josiah Clark being sweet on me gave me shivers of pleasure I couldn't have bought with a chest of gold.

It was just on the far side of the Clark farm I saw it. I sucked in my breath and gripped Old Pet's mane hard. There must have been fifty or a hundred soldiers in grey and brown with their horses tethered on a line, and scattered about stood a few tents. The soldiers seemed to be repairing their tents and other equipment. Was that Captain there? If he saw me, a Quaker girl, heading to town wouldn't he figure it out? I pulled my bonnet up over my face.

And then I felt ashamed for me and mine. These were my country's soldiers asking for their men to rise to the call of duty, like Miss Emily, my teacher said. Josiah and his family made the sacrifice, why not mine? For a moment I even felt angry and stirred enough to ride right up to Captain Garson and tell him where to find Father, Uncle Joel, Uncle George and all the Bushes, Shelburns, and Crabtrees too. I stopped Old Pet and looked down the road to the camp. I couldn't make out any one person clearly. My stomach contracted and I found myself moving Old Pet down the road to Grandfather's. All I thought about the whole way was the loving embraces I could expect from Grandma Mitchie and I blubbered like a little child.

* * *

When Grandma Mitchie saw me coming up the main road she knew I'd been crying. She stood out on the colonnade porch of her big two story house that sat on the main east-west road on the west side of the center of town. All us children called her 'Mitchie', though I never knew why; her real name was Christina. She wore a plain, grey dress, like all the old Quaker ladies, and her greying hair all tied in a bun in back. Some in the family say I favored her: short with deep, wide set green eyes separated by a nose as thin ridged as a knife blade, and a pencil line for a mouth. Father used to say I was a sensible looking child. Maybe that's when I first started getting angry with him. It wouldn't have killed him to tell me if I was beautiful. Mama told me that sometimes, but I guess I didn't believe her because I reckon she was just trying to make up for Father. But Father always snorted and said beauty was a vanity.

Well, Grandma Mitchie swept me into the house as quick as she could and into her cozy little parlor where the fire was all made up.

"Well, child, what is it that has thee so troubled?"

I answered her as best I could between sobs. "Conscriptors are after Tom Bush…Father sent me…get Uncle Joel out the way…" Somehow Grandma Mitchie understood all that. Her heavy brow (like mine) knit over with concern. She stroked my hair, bit her lip and led me upstairs to the guest bedroom I always stayed in. As she went downstairs calling Aunt Elizabeth and Aunt Sarah, I walked to the window. The sight sent a shock through me. Cavalry troopers in butternut brown and grey clattered by on horses from one end of the main road through Jonesville to the other. The whole world seemed filled with the Confederate Army. My heart felt torn first one way, then another. I could picture Josiah Clark sitting proud down there and my heart stirred, yet I feared for my Father and for all the Friends. I did the only thing I could; I kicked off my shoes and crawled under the covers of the big bed and hid.

I must have cried myself to sleep. When I woke it was dark in the room and I was terrified. I rolled out of bed and rushed out of the room in my stocking feet, desperately sure that the house would be empty, or worse yet, full of horrors, like in nightmares. At first, my nightmare seemed to be coming true. I heard no noise from the kitchen.

"Grandma!" I cried. And then a firm hand caught my shoulder from behind. I nearly fainted with fright until I heard Grandfather's voice. "Hush child. We're all in the parlor." I turned and found Grandfather Andrew standing right behind me and all of a sudden the nightmare faded. He nodded in the direction of the parlor door, his fierce blue eyes somehow dimmed and his white beard framing his round face with more lines in it than I remembered. He seemed to be holding up something heavy. I was dimly shocked; this was the man who'd stood for Virginia in the U.S. Senate. Even with the war on, folks still called him "Senator," a title he didn't care for, being a Friend. I'd always thought he stood like he was made of a single slab of slate. But he bowed a little tonight as he towered above me.

He led me through the parlor door to where the fire crackled. Aunt Elizabeth and Aunt Sarah sat on the small divan, leaning on one another and staring into the fire. Grandma Mitchie sat straight, her hands clenched, in a chair right by the fire, staring into the flames. When she saw me she opened up her arms and I ran to her embrace. I leaned against her and she said, "Thee did the best thee could child." The remark seemed mysterious, foreboding. I had to ask.

"What happened, Grandma?"

Both aunts sobbed gently and Grandfather turned away from the fire. No one seemed to want to answer. Grandma whispered, "The conscriptors caught thy Uncle Joel. Thee warned us, but we didn't reach him in time."

Traitor! Traitor! Traitor! In my mind I screamed the word at myself until it meant nothing, became a useless, animal sound. Moping along on Old Pet and just about to go betray them all to the soldiers on Clark's farm. I just knew it was all my doing and God must be punishing me for my sinful thoughts. I hated Josiah Clark and his whole family. It would be too much of a trial for me to relate the misery I felt all that night and the little sleep I got.

In the morning, a dim pall, like battle smoke, hung over my heart. Everyone at breakfast ate in silence the buckwheat griddle cakes Grandma, Aunt Elizabeth and Aunt Sarah served us. You heard every clink as metal fork scraped on porcelain plate, every creak of the old oak tree outside the kitchen window as it nodded in the chill wind. I reckon I would have gone through that breakfast without a word but for my need to know when they'd send me home.

"Grandma?" I ventured. She looked up from her plate and not until then did I notice the red lining her eyelids.

"Yes, my dear."

"Shall I go home this morning?"

She looked at Grandfather who sucked in a big breath and said, "No, child. We have already sent word to thy father in our own way. I think it best for thee to stay here till First Day and go out with us."

I found this reassuring. I dreaded the ride past the Clark farm. But I blurted out my next thought. "If we go to meeting, won't they find Father and Uncle George and the rest?"

Grandfather waited a while and shook his head. "No, they won't." And I knew he wouldn't tell me more. That was all I was allowed to know for the endless hours of that cold, windy Seventh Day. The gusts howled against the house all afternoon like lonely voices of lost Friends, dragged to their martyrs' deaths. I figured I needed to do some praying, having laid a number of sins on my soul in the last few hours. I looked out the window across Grandfather's vast fields, past the empty slave cabins that had been empty long before the war. I tried opening myself to the Inner Light, and I waited a long time, but my heart was so full of so many things I couldn't quiet myself proper like. I kept trying. Throughout the day the house was quiet, like a tomb. Dark came quickly with winter so close. I kept my station by the kitchen window, going over and over what I could have done different and each time agitating my heart more and more. So when I saw the man dash from behind the shadows of one of the empty cabins, I figured it was something the wind was doing to play tricks on my mind until it happened again. Someone was sneaking up on the house. I imagined assassins in the night, gunning us treasonous Quakers down and we, like sheep, forgiving them without lifting a hand. I wanted to scream a warning. No. It had to be the wind. I couldn't see anyone anymore. Then all of a sudden a man's face and figure pressed against the kitchen door. I screamed so loud that I thought surely I'd have a heart attack. The man let himself in swiftly through the door and clapped a hand over my mouth.

"Stop that noise!" he hissed and I realized that in my panic I hadn't recognized Uncle Joel. His clothes were ripped and muddy and he needed a shave. He smelled like damp and dank. Grandfather was in the room in a moment. His eyes grew big and he cried out softly, "Andrew Joel! Thanks be to God!" Grandfather strode over faster than thinking about it, and threw his arms around Uncle Joel, dank smell and all.

I watched the two men embrace and wondered if Father had ever embraced Grandfather this way. Seemed like when my father was with his father they stared into the distance and talked crops. This was purely new to me, to see two men unafraid to show their feelings. Boys are so stupid that way, always making out like they don't feel nothing.

Well, Grandfather didn't stand there long. "Come out of the kitchen, Joel. People can see thee through the windows. Come, Maggie." He led us into the parlor where Grandma Mitchie, Elizabeth and Sarah were poised and tense. "It's all right," he said, "God has been good and sent us back our Joel." Well, the mood in that parlor burst like a thundercloud waiting to let go its rain. Grandma and the aunts fell on Uncle Joel and covered him with kisses without a thought for his damp smell. Grandma was the first to find words. "Is thee hurt, son?"

"No, mama," Joel answered, "Just wet and hungry."

"Elizabeth, go fix thy brother a cold plate," Grandma ordered. "Sarah, go up to Joel's room and get him a shirt, some breeches and his heavy jacket. And fetch his black boots—and a hat." The aunts hurried out of the room and Grandfather made Joel sit in his own big chair. Grandma threw a quilt around him.

"Tell us what happened, son," Grandfather asked when Joel was comfortable.

"Well, they caught me coming in from the fields on Sandy Ridge, some men from the 64th Virginia. I was standing right out in the open with no horse, so I didn't stand no chance. They tied my hands and marched me and some other fellows over towards the Clark farm up Long Hollow and I began worrying if they got Henry and George."

"No," Grandfather shook his head. "Maggie saw them chasing Tom Bush and spread the word. She came here to give us warning, but they caught thee before I could send word. Sid seen them leading thee off. Maggie's been quite a little hero."

Joel smiled at me and I felt so ashamed I wanted to run out of the room. If they only knew what was going on in my heart they wouldn't think me much of a hero. Joel didn't seem to notice. I guess he thought me a hero too, even though I hadn't done him no good. Just then, Elizabeth and Sarah came in with the food and clothes. Uncle Joel got himself dressed and wolfed down the cold chicken on his plate, trying to talk all at the same time.

"Well, they come to the bridge over the Town Fork, and you know that bridge is narrow and with the ice on it, mighty slippery. So they decided to send us over one at a time. I went first. They untied my hands and sent me over, telling me they'd shoot me if I tried anything. Well, the water was pretty high and moving fast. I thought I just might freeze, but I figured I could dive deep enough for the water to deflect their bullets. I made like I tripped and dived as best I could on the downstream side. I heard the rifles, but by that time I was in the water. Lord, it was mighty cold. When I got out, they wasn't anywhere near, but I was careful. When I got here this morning, I saw some of them watching the house and I hid and waited till they left. I reckon they got hungry and gave it up or figured I headed a different way."

By this time Joel was all dressed and the food was gone.

"What will we do?" Grandma asked, touching the side of her face lightly in a gesture of worry.

"Thee can't stay here, not one night," Grandfather announced with finality, shaking his head.

"Andrew!" Grandma protested.

"No, Christina," he replied, "He's not safe here. Son, does thee remember the Williams family that came up the road before the war from the North Carolina Meeting?"

"Yes, Papa," Joel nodded.

"Well, I have their letters. They've found a fine farm and meeting in Indiana. Thy brother George has already left today for the Gap. The Union Army there will send him to the Williamses. Thee must go after him."

Grandfather's words sent a chill over the whole room. The thought of Uncle Joel and Uncle George two states away and leaving tonight was as solemn as a death or a wedding.

Grandma was finally able to say, "No. My son, oh..."

Uncle Joel hugged her and said, "Papa's right, Mama. I have got to go while I still can."

I never saw Grandma before this when she wasn't strong and sure, but for a moment there she just let Uncle Joel hold her. Without thinking about it, I went over and hugged her too.

"Now," Grandfather sighed, "If we could only get Henry to go with thee." He looked at me and said, "Thy father, child, is the most stubborn creature on God's green earth."

Grandfather rarely said things in judgment of other people, especially his own family, so I knew he was angry. But if Father was stubborn, he learned it from Grandfather. Why hadn't he learned kindness and love from Grandfather while he was at it?

"I best go now," Uncle Joel said, gently detaching himself from Grandma. He embraced Elizabeth and Sarah, and even me. Then he shook Grandfather's hand and they embraced one more time. Grandfather was even crying. I saw the wetness beneath his eyes and I'd never seen a man do that before. It didn't seem so silly as it might sound. He released Joel and held his shoulders, saying, "Remember what I've taught thee: never raise a gun against any man, my son. He never did thee any harm."

Uncle Joel nodded his agreement and moved to the door so fast it took me awhile to realize he had slipped out into the night and was gone.

III
Meeting Day

By First Day morning, I was so agitated that I threw up twice and was unable to eat. I fully expected us to be seized by the army and thrown into prison as the traitors we were. But not even the army of the Confederate States of America was going to stop Grandfather from going to meeting on First Day. Before the war, Grandfather had plenty of help around the plantation, for the slaves he freed came back to work for him for pay, as freemen. He housed them well and gave them land, seed, chickens and pigs to get started, and they worked for him like only a free man can. He even sat down and ate with them, something no white man in Jonesville ever did. The folks in town thought he was crazy, but Grandfather told me that every man has the Inner Light of God inside them, and it was sin to enslave a brother. Grandfather was Quaker right down to the ground.

But with the secession of Virginia, Grandfather's field hands fled North with their families, fearful that they might be enslaved again. I couldn't blame them for fearing it. So that just left Sid, the orphan boy Grandfather had taken in off the streets, and Joel to help around the place. With Joel gone, Sid and Grandfather had to hitch the horse into the rig by themselves. Grandfather went to it without a word of complaint. Instead he laid aside his coat, rolled up his sleeves and thanked God that he was still strong enough to put a horse in harness. Then he hitched Old Pet to the back. It took longer, but we loaded up the buckboard and headed to my home in Long Hollow.

The one thing that wasn't proper Quaker about my family is that they didn't live close to one of the established Quaker meeting houses. The nearest one was two day's ride down to Lost Creek, in Jefferson County, Tennessee. And with the war on, even that was too much to get to. So with the handful of other Quaker families in the county, wc took turns holding meeting in different houses. Most often, it was at Grandfather's plantation, but this First Day meeting was scheduled to take place at my house.

Normally, I would be home to help Mama with the cleaning and the setting out the chairs in the parlor, but nothing had been normal since last Sixth Day when Caleb Pennington announced the war to me. I sat on the bed of the wagon between Aunt Elizabeth and Aunt Sarah, watching Old Pet work to follow us. I felt deathly ill and fully expected for us to be stopped and arrested.

Aunt Sarah was a small woman, and like Elizabeth, of marrying age, and even almost past it. She had golden hair and big, beautiful eyes that made men look at her. She was real pretty. She sat on my left and looked out at the fields go by in the fresh wind with the low orange sun bathing us all in fiery light. Aunt Elizabeth was taller and plainer, with brown curls, a button nose and round cheeks. Men didn't look at her so much and I think that was a trial to her. She sat on my right. After twenty minutes went by of listening to meadowlarks, seeing as I wasn't very talkative, Sarah and Elizabeth struck up a conversation.

"There's the Hobbs place," Sarah sighed.

"Oh, now stop. Jason Hobbs is too old and he's no Friend," Elizabeth chided.

"Hush, 'Lizbeth. Thee knows there's not a marriageable Friend 'tween Tennessee and Indiana. Thee may wish to be an old maid, but I still have hopes."

"Papa would be mighty troubled to hear thee talk that way, sister. And what if Jason Hobbs ever did work up the courage to loosen his tongue and ask thee?"

Sarah thought about this awhile and I almost stopped breathing to hear what she would say. There was a joy in knowing that I wasn't the only one in the family that had notions of forsaking the faith in my marriage. "Well," Sarah replied, "I reckon it wouldn't hurt none to listen to him."

"Sarah Milbourn. May God forgive thee," Elizabeth snorted.

"Oh hush, 'Lizbeth. I'm sure God isn't as joyless as thee makes him out to be. If'n he wanted me to marry a Friend, I'm sure there'd be one to ask me. As it is, I'll take what the good Lord sends with thanks. Surely thee would like to have a husband and little ones? This war's been going on three years now with no end in sight." She brushed her blond hair from her face and I could see she was troubled. "I don't see no end to it at all. There ain't no Friends passing through from North Carolina like there used to be. Maybe Joel should have taken us with him to Indiana."

"Lord, Sarah, I don't mean the Almighty don't want us to marry. But to marry a man not a Friend? Why it'd be leaving the Faith."

"Reckon so. But we ain't proper Friends anyway."

"Sarah, whatever does thee mean?"

"Well, here we are, not living near no regular meeting. We could have moved down to Tennessee or across the river to Indiana before the war, but Papa, Henry and George won't leave this country."

"How thee does talk, sister," Elizabeth huffed.

"All right, sister. Answer me true. If Roger Sinclair ever stepped from behind the counter of his store and fell on his knee to thee, would thee refuse him?"

I hadn't heard about Aunt Elizabeth being sweet on Mr. Sinclair.

"Well," Elizabeth said, "I reckon it wouldn't hurt none to listen to him."

My aunts fell silent just as we passed by the Clark place. I closed my hands into fists and fought the urge to cry. You could just see the cone shaped tents and the smoke from cooking fires. I listened for the sound of hooves. No mounted party in grey came up the road to stop us.

Coming up the drive of my father's farm felt odd to me, as if I were going to a stranger's house and not the only home I could remember. The house looked no different and yet somehow different, with its two stories and shingle roof that came right down over the porches that ran all the way around the house. Far across the fields, a ribbon of blue which was the Powell River ran at the far side of Father's land. In between, corn and oat fields swept down to the river like a bright quilt, dotted with orange pumpkins. Other wagons stood parked in front of the house. We were late on account of Grandfather's and Sid's hitching. My aunties helped me down from the wagon bed. I was weak with hunger, but the thought of food made me ill.

Grandma Mitchie led me by the hand into our large, wood beamed parlor. It was set very simply and always the same. Maybe a dozen chairs were set on one side and a dozen on the other with an aisle up the middle. Two chairs were set up front and through the door beyond that, Mama's kitchen and dining room. I could smell the bacon from breakfast still. The women always sat together on the right side and the men on the left. Any visiting preacher would be welcome to the front chairs.

When we walked in I saw Mrs. Shelburn, Mrs. Crabtree, Mrs. Bush, Mama, and Aunt Mary on the women's side, just like usual. I was stunned to see Mr. Crabtree, Mr. Shelburn, Mr. Bush and Father sitting on the men's side like there were no conscriptors out looking for them. At least Tom Bush, Uncle George, and Uncle Joel had the sense not to show up to where every soul in Lee County knew the Quakers could be found on First Day morning. I suppose Mr. Shelburn was safe enough, being an older man, but I'd expected the men's side to be almost empty.

I reckon Grandfather did too, because he looked thunderstruck. He walked up the aisle and leaned over to say some words softly to Father. I'd never seen him so forceful with Father before. I couldn't make out what he said, but it wasn't gentle. Nobody else except maybe Grandma dared ever take such a tone with Father. But Father sat there like a statue, shaking his head no. Grandma, the aunties and I went over and sat next to Mama. Mama gave me a firm hug that made me feel better. I knew she was glad to see me and worried too. But my safety was only half her worry now. I could tell by the way she kept glancing over at Father that she thought he ought to be hiding too. I guessed they'd probably had words, but of course, Father had his way in the end. I don't remember one time when he did one thing that wasn't his own idea right down the line. My father was like a rock, no doubt about it.

Well, the meeting started, that is, everyone sat down and fell silent. There wasn't no music in Friend's meetings. We didn't have nothing to get between us in listening to the Inner Light. If the Spirit of God moved someone to speak, then they stood up and spoke. But in our little meeting, there wasn't much speaking. None of us, except maybe Grandma, had the gift of preaching. We were used to Friends on the road having someone who was a preacher. So generally, we sat there for an hour in quiet and listened to our own Inner Light.

Sometimes I thought I could hear something, but for the most part I spent First Day mornings thinking about all my worries and joys. I don't think the Lord thought much of my devotion. But when I told Grandma Mitchie, she told me not to worry, that God loved me and would touch my heart in His own time. That particular First Day, all I could think of was the army, Josiah

Clark, and the sick ache in my belly. I started to settle down some after about a half an hour when I heard horses's hooves all around the house. Then I started shivering so violently that Mama held me tight.

Men's voices rang outside the house and the lowing of our cows nearly drowned them out. The parlor door crashed open and there stood Captain Garson, grimacing at us all. I thought my heart would fail. It was my worst nightmare come true; I couldn't get no lower. He looked around the room and his eyes lit on me for what seemed like forever. I could have died right there and not felt a thing. Mama clutched me tight, I reckon without knowing she was doing it.

"Well, well, well," Captain Garson said, "What have we here? Which one of you is Henry Milbourn?"

Father stood up slowly and turned to face Captain Garson.

"I am."

"Under the law of the Confederate States of America I'm expropriating your cattle and the corn in your cribs for use by the quartermaster of the 64th Virginia Cavalry, Confederate States Army."

I expected Father to argue, but he just nodded real slow, like he was being told tomorrow's weather.

"Forgive me," Captain Garson went on in a voice overly polite, "if I am interrupting your sabbath, but there is the matter of another law duty compels me to enforce. By the authority of the Conscription Act of 1862, I arrest all men here present at or under the age of forty-five for service in the Confederate States Army. Please come along peaceable, the house is surrounded."

Mr. Shelburn stood up. "But what about the exemption for Friends?"

"That exemption, " Captain Garson replied coolly, "is granted for Quakers who support the war with material help. I can find no record, sir, of any of the men here supporting the war in any way."

Father spoke up, his voice shaking, much to my surprise. "But what about our farms and our families? What will they eat?"

Captain Garson thought a second, pulled out his pocket watch and clicked open the cover. "I'll give you five minutes to arrange something with your neighbors here." He stepped out of the house and closed the door.

Father looked at Mama, who let go of me and ran to hold him. Other wives went to their husbands, stood close and talked in low voices and then altogether. I felt panic building in my breast. Grandma, Elizabeth and Sarah held onto William, little Mary, Robert and baby John. Little Mary was crying and I looked away from her to keep from crying too. I don't know why I didn't cry just then. Maybe it was because I felt that things couldn't get no worse and somehow there was a calm in that fact; there wasn't nothing left to lose. Father came over with Mama, arms around each other and Mama's face tear-streaked.

"Children. Thy Father's got to go away for awhile. I'm counting on you all to be strong, 'specially you, Maggie. Thee is the eldest and thy mother's support. Mrs. Shelburn will be staying here on the farm. You're to obey her as you would me or thy mother. Understand?"

I nodded, feeling a knot in my throat. And suddenly I felt guilty for ever having been angry with Father. I ran over and embraced him around the waist. He did not embrace me back. He didn't seem to know I'd even hugged him. If he'd kicked me in the face, I couldn't have been more stung. And that's when I really started crying.

Captain Garson came through the door, gesturing outside with his arm. "Gentlemen?" he said just as casual as if inviting them outside for a cigar.

Father moved away and Mama clung to him saying, "The Lord shield thee, Henry." He nodded like she was asking him to milk the cows and stepped to the door without a word. Oh, I hated him, the cold, unfeeling shirker. I was glad they were taking him, who felt so little for us. Why didn't he fight? Why didn't he protest? Why didn't he even try to stay with us? I hardly believed I'd heard him ask Captain Garson about what was going to happen to us. The man had no feelings and I hated the sight of him. Still, why was I crying?

We women all followed them outside, Grandfather being the only man they didn't take. Soldiers in butternut and grey stood all around the house and the barn. Captain Garson wasn't bluffing; there was no escape. Some soldiers tied Father's and Mr. Bush's, Mr. Shelburn's, and Mr. Crabtree's hands. Then they pushed our men up on horses and led them away at a walk holding the reins so our men had no way to control the horses. I guessed they'd learned from losing Uncle Joel in the Town Fork. Other soldiers drove away our cows. Mrs. Shelburn, a broad, elderly woman in grey cotton and white bonnet walked up to where Captain Garson mounted his horse.

"Soldier," she addressed him, not knowing his name and like a Quaker, refusing to name him by titles of special respect. He didn't care for this, I could tell by his face. She went on, "What of the children? Will thee not leave one milk cow for them?"

Captain Garson grimaced again and barked at one of the soldiers driving our cattle, "Sergeant!"

"Yessir!"

"Leave these people one milk cow!"

"Yessir!" The sergeant cut out Flora, Mama's favorite cow and drove her back toward us.

"I thank thee," Mrs. Shelburn said stiffly and picking up a stick, drove Flora back into the near empty barn. I watched Father and the other men enfolded in the mass of soldiers and disappear down the road, and then without knowing what I was doing, I found myself plunging down the road after them, screaming, "Papa! Papa! Papa!" Yet, they rode away at a canter and soon I all could see of them was dust up the road. I slowed and stopped, my feet clomping heavily like dead weights. I turned and looked back to our farm. Mama was coming up the road after me as fast as she could go. I ran to her, and when I reached her, I buried my face in her dress and let all my feelings out.

IV

Switching Sides Again

I think I would have sooner risked dying and going to Hell than going to school that Second Day morning. I knew as sure as spring followed winter that every person in Lee County knew by now that the army had seized the local Quaker men. And every eye would be on William and me once we reached school. If they'd only stared at us, that would be awful enough, but I feared after Caleb Pennington's mud attack, that there would be more of the same.

"Mama, I feel ill after yesterday…" I pleaded. It sounded reasonable enough. We stood in the kitchen by the dining room door with Mrs. Shelburn in her tent sized apron, sitting at the table with the little ones. Mama was cooking greens and baking cornbread. I figured she was only paying me half attention anyway, and that I'd get a half thought answer. But she surprised me, pulling out the bread pan with the cotton mitts and letting it clatter down on top of the cooling rack. Then she turned to me and her eyes were filled with something I didn't often see there; it was half way between crying and shouting. She knelt down and held my shoulders.

"Maggie, dear. I know thee is sorely vexed by everything that's happened, but we must go on. Father would want us to. If we start hanging our heads around the county and hide ourselves, why, it would be like telling everybody they are right about us. To go on living our normal lives is our testimony to the truth of the Lord. Can thee understand that, my love?"

I didn't understand it at all. I wasn't even sure we were right. But I'd have done a lot rather than let her down just then, even go to school. I nodded like I understood. Within the hour, William and I were fed, bundled, and walking up Long Hollow Road. The frosty morning air bit at my ears and nose and our steps seemed loud enough to wake the dead. We didn't talk. William and I both knew we were thinking the same thing. And on top of that, I was trying very hard not to think about what Josiah Clark would say. Along the way I picked up a rock. It wasn't a very Quaker thing to do, I reckon, but I was bound and determined to respond this time. Father always quoted to us, "he who lives by the sword will die by the sword." I reckon that was fine with me. It was a better fate than being laughed to death. I worked the rock in my fist over and over, revolving the grit and the sharp edges around and around, pressing them into the flesh of my hand.

Finally, I saw the low log building around the curve in the road and heard the laughter and shouting of our schoolmates. My throat got tight; my heart nearly beat out of my chest, but my legs kept walking and the rock in my fist got heavier.

And suddenly we were there and they were all looking at us, just like I knew they would. It was so still that I distinctly heard the crunching of old leaves under my feet. I tightened up every muscle in my body, ready for the first word. Whoever said it was going to get my rock right in their big mouth. Josiah Clark, leaning against a tree, walked over. Lord Jesus no. Not Josiah. I couldn't throw the rock at him. But I steeled my resolve. Even if sweet Josiah turned on me, he'd be the first to feel this Quaker girl's mettle. I wanted to be dead and right quick—it would have been a mite easier.

"Morning, Maggie," he said and I could not make up my mind whether he was being cheery or sarcastic. I stopped, but I didn't lift my head. The rock felt warm in my hand.

"Heard your pap joined the army."

I nodded, waiting for the mocking voices to begin, waiting for the first shot in my doomed war.

"I bet you're right proud of him."

I looked up in astonishment at his face. He actually meant it! I couldn't believe it. He had to know; everybody knew. Yet his face was smiling and sincere. Josiah Clark knew my father had been dragged to the army and here he was making it sound honorable. No, it couldn't be true.

Caleb Pennington shouted, "Yeah, and they had to take him tied up like an ol' hog."

My fist clenched, ready to fire. Josiah turned and gave Caleb a withering look. Caleb clamed up fast. The others in the schoolyard looked away, afraid to offend Josiah. It was true.

I heard myself stammer, "Yes, thank thee." I'm sure William thought I was just playing along, but the idea seemed real to me. Josiah was absolutely right. My father was finally doing his duty to my country and I was at least in part, I guess, happy to see it.

Still, the tension there in the yard was as thick as river mud. I reckon we were all relieved when Miss Emily stepped out the door and rang the handbell. We filed in right quiet for us, but Miss Emily didn't seem to notice. She smiled at me and William with kindness and I knew that she knew too.

It would be no exaggeration to say that I loved Miss Emily. She was a short woman, no more than twenty-five, I reckon, with straight brown hair and small, twinkly eyes. She wasn't a beauty, but she had a glow about her that couldn't be mistaken. To listen to her teach was like hearing a story told around the fire. And best of all, she gave me books to read and taught me songs. In our house the only books were the Bible and George Fox's sermons. But Miss Emily loaned me *The Pathfinder* and *Jane Eyre* and it had opened a whole new, beautiful world for me, where there was song and sunshine and laughter and adventures, and people were happy like I never knew. This world was full of people who never read George Fox and did mostly as they pleased. These people had real book-learning. I wanted that world, even if it was a sin, I wanted it with all my soul. In the moment when I'd decided not to marry a Friend, I realized the man I'd marry would just have to have book learning.

In the school house we all sat on benches while Miss Emily sat up front and taught the lessons. It reminded me a little of meeting with the boys sitting on one side and us on the other. That morning as the other students scuffled through the dust on the floor, the other girls sat far away from me. Josiah sat by William, who looked uncomfortable some with the attention. When Miss Emily came in, I trembled. What would she say? Would she mention anything about my father?

"Children, as we'll be having a visitor later, we'll put off ciphering today and begin with our reading lessons." I breathed a sigh of relief. For most of the children, this meant getting out their readers, dull stories written about children learning to behave, which they would have to read aloud, one by one to Miss Emily. My reading skills had long since passed beyond the highest of readers and this meant I had the privilege to select a novel from Miss Emily's desk. The day she first let me read, she'd asked if my parents would object. I honestly answered, "No," for there was no chance that I would ever tell them, especially Father. I think Miss Emily knew that too. But she didn't want to cause no trouble with Father. Miss Emily and I understood each other right well.

Right then I dived for a good hour into Jane Eyre's world, into Thornfield Hall and under the gaze of the dashing Mr. Rochester. There I was safe for a time from the world where I was a double traitor. Occasionally, if the sun was coming just right through the door, it sent up a little ray of weak, winter light, like a stairway to the Almighty's Throne. I would look up from my reading and watch this light from time to time and always feel a great stirring in my heart like the joy I felt the day Josiah walked me home. Jane was making herself at home in Thornfield after being at an awful school and I was making myself at home here in the school after being so tight bound at home. A plan, or maybe more of a desire, began to push its way to the front of my mind.

I think I would have abandoned it again quickly, but at that moment Captain Garson splashed through my beam of winter light at the door and strode in with his heavy boots clumping on the squeaky floor boards. I think I jumped with surprise and fear of this man who made my blood run cold, but nobody saw it. Every eye fell on Captain Garson. Captain Garson's eyes fell on Miss Emily with a look of affection no one could mistake. It was a look Mr. Rochester might have given to Jane. I think all of the girls in the school house sighed in unison just under their breath. When Miss Emily looked up at him, the love shone in her eyes. He walked over to her desk, where she'd been sitting listening to Rafe Courtland murdering his reader. She rose with his hand and stood with him front and center.

"Children, I want you to meet Captain Garson, my fiancé. Jonathan," she said, looking in his eyes, "this is my class."

Captain Garson touched the brim of his hat, "Pleased to make your acquaintance." His eyes swept the room and stopped on me, "and your re-acquaintance."

We were all thunderstruck. None of us could speak. My heart fluttered between joy and fear. Miss Emily laughed with delight. "Why children, if I'd known this could get you all quiet so fast I would have tried it sooner. Jonathon and I are going to marry later this month at the First Methodist Episcopal Church. I shall be very sorry to leave you all."

Everybody knew that married ladies didn't teach school and there was no other teacher in Long Hollow. Caleb Pennington was smiling, but I knew that was because he figured on not having to go to school no more. I could see that Captain Garson was really as dashing as Mr. Rochester, but I couldn't forget all the horrible things I had thought about him. I shivered at the thought of what he might have told Miss Emily about me and mine. And I resolved right then and there, to go through with my plan.

"I'm giving you a half holiday today," Miss Emily smiled. The class cheered and gathered around Miss Emily and Captain Garson, except for Caleb Pennington and some of the other boys, who tumbled out through the door. Now or never. I stood up to where Josiah was standing just back of the ring of girls and boldly whispered in his ear. "Will thee. . .you wait for me and walk me home?"

He turned, surprise in his face and smiled. I went over to where William waited. "Go home. Tell Mama I'll be home after I've talked to Miss Emily." Well, it wasn't entirely a lie. I did plan to say something to Miss Emily too. William gave me a puzzled look, shrugged and headed out the door. When he'd gone, I stood right next to Josiah like I wasn't shy and waited with him for our turn. I got all tingly just doing what I wanted instead of being shy. I tried not to think of what Father would say, and power of making my own decision was delicious in every way. I thought I just might get used to the taste and never give it up. When the Johnston girls curtseyed and left, there was Josiah and me facing Miss Emily and Captain Garson. For a moment there was a look in his face of mild surprise at my boldness. Yes, let him think that of me instead of the other. Miss Emily leaned down and kissed me on the cheek.

"Jonathan," she said, "Maggie here is my finest scholar. I have great hopes for her."

"Well," he said, raising his eyebrows in pretended surprise, "I am very pleased to hear it. I apologize Miss Maggie if I and my men disrupted your Sabbath yesterday. I want you to know I'm a God fearing man and I only did my duty."

Well, I looked down at the floor when no words came, but then I got angry with myself and I hated every shy part of me. I looked him straight in the eye and said, "Thank you, sir," as bold as a newborn calf. He smiled in delight and I felt accepted by all these people.

"And don't worry about your father, Miss Maggie," Captain Garson added. "He'll settle down to soldiering soon enough. Come see him anytime."

"Thank you, sir," I said, but I wasn't sure I wanted to see Father "settling down." It all got quiet, like everybody wanted to say something but nobody could think of nothing. I realized I was still holding Miss Emily's copy of *Jane Eyre* and I held it out to her to take. She hesitated a moment and opened her mouth as if to say something. Then she took the book and leaning down over her desk, took up her quill pen and wrote something in it. When she stood up again she handed it to me.

"Here, Maggie. I want you to have this, that is, if your mother will allow."

I reached out slowly and took it from her. I couldn't have waited if my life had depended on it. I opened it up and read.

"To Maggie Milbourn, my finest student,

My hopes and wishes go with you. I hope you
will finish your education and be a tribute
to all of us in Long Hollow. Maybe someday
I'll send my children to your school.

Love,
Emily Tanner Garson"

Tanner was her last name, but I guess she figured she'd be Garson soon enough. The book trembled in my hand. I think I managed to whisper, "Thank you." Then Josiah, of course, said light and breezy, like we'd been talking about crops, "Well, Maggie and I best be going. Good day to you, ma'am, sir."

"I'll see you in the morning," Miss Emily said. Then they smiled at him and a wonderful thing happened: Josiah took my hand right in front of them and led me out of the school room. I think I blushed two tones of red. He didn't let go neither, once we were outside and walking through the frosty air down the lane. I was almost afraid to move my hand in case he took it to mean I wanted to stop holding hands. But I still had enough boldness to say, "Josiah, I want thee, I mean, I want you to do me a favor." I almost gagged to hear how forward I sounded.

"Surely, Maggie."

"Can...you...help me to learn to talk like regular folks around here? If I talk to...you enough, I figure I can learn it."

"T'would be a pleasure," he laughed. "And you come on down to the farm and visit your pa any time." That thought sapped my boldness right fast. Josiah seemed to sense this.

"Don't worry none about your pa resisting, Maggie. I don't blame you for it."

If he had lifted a death sentence from me, I couldn't have been more relieved. Then I did the boldest thing of all. I leaned over and kissed him on the cheek faster than it takes to tell it and ran off down the road hearing him laughing. He yelled, "See you tomorrow." I waved back and skipped down the road happier than I could remember being in a long while.

Even a quarter mile from my house I could see Mrs. Shelburn standing in the kitchen garden that she'd started, washed in the half-hearted midday winter sun. She looked up from her hoeing and leaned on the handle. "Well, good morning to thee, Maggie. I hear thy schoolmistress called a half holiday. Thy mother is waiting for thee inside."

Somehow the words seemed heavy and dark. Folks didn't usually tell you your father or mother was waiting for you inside unless there was something to tell, something too hard to say right out. I walked in the house a little slower, taking time to stash *Jane Eyre* in the folds of my dress. Everything seemed like I'd left it that morning. Little Mary, Rob and William played with wooden dolls on the floor and baby John rocked in his cradle breathing quiet, only the hinge squeaking. Mama stood at the kitchen table packing food into a large basket. She looked up when I came through the door.

"There thee is. Come here, Maggie. Can thee carry this or is it too heavy?"

I tried lifting the stuffed basket off the table. It took some doing, but I could lift it all right.

"Well," Mama said, frowning, "I'll send William with thee to help thee carry it."

"Carry it where, Mama?"

She turned and stoked the fire on the hearth, absorbed in her work, so I couldn't see her face as she answered, "To thy father. The regiment is over on the Clark farm I hear. Thee knows the Clark boy, doesn't thee?"

My whole body stiffened and a chill went over me, though the kitchen was warm. If she'd asked me to parade through the center of Jonesville with a sign around my neck announcing me as a traitor, I don't think I'd be any more unwilling. I was ready to scream no, ready to take any punishment for defiance she could think up when Mama turned away from the fire and I could see that she'd been crying, little streaks running down her cheeks. Next thing I remember I was walking out the door with the basket and William watching it like he expected me to drop it any moment. Every scratch of my footsteps up that road sounded loud enough to wake the dead.

When we reached the lane up to the Clark farm, I hesitated. I'd thought up at least two good excuses by that point: what if the soldiers just took the food? Wouldn't that be a waste of what little we had? And what if giving Father special treatment made the other soldiers dislike him more than they must already, he being a Quaker? All sorts of bad possibilities flashed through my head, but the thought of my mother's anguish kept my feet picking up and putting down, almost without my permission, up the Clark farm lane. A ways on at a place where two old oaks leaned across the road from each side like a door, a sentry in butternut stepped out with an old squirrel gun and a saber swinging from his hip. William and I froze.

"Halt. What do you want here?" Another sentry, a younger fellow in a dirty grey uniform appeared from behind the other oak.

I swallowed the lump in my throat. "Please, mister. I come to bring some vittles to our father."

The first sentry squinted. "What's his name?"

"Henry Milbourn."

The second sentry scoffed, "Shoot, Jesse, that's one of them bellyachin' Quakers."

"Clear off," the first sentry said, "Ain't no privileges for those fellers."

Why didn't I just do what he said? Mama would have understood. It was the perfect excuse. But the way he said it riled me. I heard something out of me cry, "But Captain Garson told me we could visit our father!" Well, both of those soldiers got a worried look on their face. The older one said, "Go on, Jimmy, get the Captain and see what he says." Then to me he said, "You wait here and we'll see if you're lying." The power of that one name seemed impressive to me. Among the Friends, we all avoid trying to be more important than anyone else. I put the basket down and William held my hand. The first sentry eyed the basket hungrily. I just knew he expected me to bribe him, but I wasn't just a Quaker girl. I had powerful friends. In a few minutes Captain Garson and the young sentry came up. As soon as he saw me he smiled and waved me on to go to him. I picked up my basket and my brother's hand and walked right past that old sentry. I could hear the other younger one complaining to Captain Garson.

"...and all them vittles for that Quaker feller..."

Captain Garson cut him short, "That herd of cattle that come in Sunday all come from that Quaker feller's farm, so quit your bellyaching. Unless there's a battle going on, this little girl can come on the post anytime she wants, y'hear?"

"Yessir."

I gave the young sentry a little smile that let him know that I forgave him his ignorance. He scowled back.

"If you'll follow me, Miss Maggie," Captain Garson said, and he led me silently through the tents where lean soldiers lay about chewing tobacco and arguing or playing cards. They all looked up when William and I came by and I think I wouldn't have been able to face that without Captain Garson leading the way. The smell of smoke and beef cooking came up from many fires where chunks of meat broiled. I figured that was what was left of our herd. Finally, after crossing the tent city we came to the Clark house. I saw Josiah's mother on the porch with a basket of laundry. She looked more tired than I remembered seeing her. She glared at me and I turned my face away. Where was Josiah? I'd have been a might more comfortable if he'd been there to make things all right. Captain Garson led me around the house to the old wash-house. I expected to see more tents but there wasn't anything there but the old wash-house with two sentries guarding the door.

Captain Garson stopped, "Bring out Private Milbourn," he ordered.

A shock reeled through me. Father was in the guardhouse. At the window of the wash-house, covered over with chicken wire, I saw the faces I knew so well from First Day meeting: Mr. Bush, Mr. Shelburn, and Mr. Crabtree. Then the sentries opened the door and Father stepped out. I almost fainted.

V
The End of School

He'd only been gone a day, but he looked like he'd been gone ten years. His clothes were ripped and soiled and his face stubbly. His wrists were red and raw. He looked at me with a hollowness in his eyes that frightened me worse than seeing a ghost. But his look at me was searching and I could see the pain in those eyes. For a moment I was sure that he saw every treacherous thought in my heart and had heard me every time I'd sinned and uttered the word 'you.' I almost turned around and ran, but I know why I didn't. As he stood there wordless, staring at me, I saw in his hollow eyes that he was more than grateful to see me and William. He needed us; he needed me. I desperately wanted him to look at me like that. Captain Garson spoke, "Well, Private. Your family has sent some vittles. You can divide them with your friends. Colonel Slemp has decided since you men won't carry a gun, you can do all the cooking and keep up the camp. But you'd better watch your mouth or y'all will wind up in the guardhouse again." Then to the sentries he said, "Let 'em out. Show 'em to the cook tent. Let Milbourn talk to his children, first." Then Captain Garson tipped his hat to me and was gone. I feared that Father would know me for a traitor for that, but when I looked at him, he wasn't angry at me at all. For a long moment I wondered if I would have to 'make conversation', but Father spoke first.

"Glad to see thee, Maggie, and thee, William," and he took the basket out of my hands. "How is thy mother?"

"She cries," I said, "but she's..." I got lost for words. 'Fine?' No. 'All right?' No, not that either. I felt flustered. Father just nodded. Suddenly a thought charged across my mind and out of my mouth before I could throw a halter on it and tie it up.

"Father, why do they have thee in the guardhouse?" I expected him to glare as he did when asked a question he didn't like. Instead, he looked into the distance and said real slow. "I have spoken what the Spirit has given me to say, spoken against violence. For that and refusing to bear arms they put us in here. But it is to be counted a joy to suffer for our Master, Maggie. Never forget that."

What did that make me? I didn't want to do no suffering at all. I wanted people to like me, to like us. Why couldn't we be normal? Miss Emily and Josiah Clark and even Captain Garson believed in Jesus and they were fighting for the country. But I couldn't tell that to Father, not ever. He wouldn't have heard me no more than he heard a bird singing outside his door. The words would have gone by him but he wouldn't catch them.

"How's the farm? Everybody?"

"They're in poor spirits, but Mrs. Shelburn's planted a garden and we still have the corn thee hid." I said the last words in a whisper.

Father's eyes flashed at me. This was more the angry man I knew. But it passed and he said, "Tell everyone to keep praying that the Lord will send us release..." I think he wanted to say more, but the sentry came back and latched onto his arm.

"All right, Milbourn. Time's up. Cook tent is that o'way." Then Father looked at me again with a longing to stay. I ran over and embraced him around the waist. The sentry pryed me off with great effort. Father stood there stiffly. I choked back all my feelings. Father turned and walked away from William and me without another look, another word.

"Father!" I screamed, but he did not turn. I wanted to run, to tell him he was a fool fighting a fool's war, but I held it all in. I didn't even cry no more. I turned, took William's hand and walked right off that farm, and I never did see Josiah. Maybe it was Father's blood running in my veins, but I could be a stone wall too. My heart, so uncertain till then, became as much a rock as his. I said little at home, but Mama and Mrs. Shelburn were too busy to notice. I went to school and read *Jane Eyre* and dreamed. Then Josiah'd walk me home and I'd talk like normal folks till I got home and hid my book. Mama would send me and William to visit Father. I'd go without a word and find him in the camp kitchen behind the stove or sometimes in the guardhouse again. He'd ask if the family was all right and I'd nod. But I couldn't bring myself to say a word to him and there was never that light in his eye any other time I visited. When I got home, I went to bed early with a new candle and read secretly more of the world of Thornfield Hall and the romantic Mr. Rochester till I couldn't keep my eyes open. This went on for four days, only the third day was marked with a pitiful Thanksgiving dinner with Mrs. Shelburn, my brothers and sister and Mama and me.

On Seventh Day, or Saturday, I went in the morning, but aside from that the visit wasn't no different. He hardly had a word for me, nor did he look me in the eye.

I don't know how much longer I could have done that. But I didn't get to find out. On Meeting Day, Mama hitched Old Pet to the wagon and we all went over to the Bush's farm for Meeting. The Bush's parlor looked mighty bare with nothing but us womenfolk and Grandfather sitting over by himself. The meeting wasn't so bad; it was routine, and that made me feel good. But I remember thinking that war couldn't get much worse than this. I was wrong.

As we drove home from the Bush's that morning, the thundering of hooves sounded on the road behind us. My heart leaped into my mouth. I sat on the bed of the buckboard with the other children huddled around me under a feeble winter sun. The wheels rattled and banged over ruts in the frozen mud, but not from the speed of our wagon; Old Pet was slow as molasses at the best of times. All the little children clutched me as the first horsemen appeared around the bend behind us.

I recognized Colonel Slemp in his white hat and yellow sash, leading the column of butternut and grey horsemen. Right up behind him rode Major Pridemore and Captain Garson. Mama pulled our wagon over to the right side of the road and the column of horsemen trotted briskly past us, their sabers, pistols, canteens and spurs all clattering like the racket of the Devil himself. Their faces bore into my soul; grim faces and determined, looking straight forward. Hands clenched reins tight, as tight as their eyes. Death was written on them as clear as handwriting. These were my country's army. These were my soldiers. I turned away so as not to see. The dust and grit filled my eyes and mouth, even after the last of them had gone. When they were out of sight and their sound died to an echo in the woods, Mrs. Shelburn said, "Lord, forgive them, for they know not what they do."

I thought of the look in their faces. They knew. Oh, yes they knew.

Mrs. Shelburn broke my thought. "Sister Mary, there's a battle brewing nearby. Best get the young'uns inside and down the cellar."

"I didn't see Henry or any of the others," Mama said, looking far away down the road.

"No, I reckon thy man is as strong a Christian soul as ever bore witness. It's as Maggie says. Come along now. Give me the reins." And Mrs. Shelburn took the reins from Mama and slapped them on Old Pet's rump. With Mrs. Shelburn at the reins, Old Pet gave a better performance. We reached home quickly. As we stepped off the wagon bed, I heard the popping of gunfire in the distance. It sounded like lots of little boys throwing rocks as hard as they could against the side of a barn. Pop! Pop!

Mrs. Shelburn put up Old Pet in the barn in a singular hurry and Mama hustled us into the house and down into the root cellar. Once down below, the sounds of the fighting became muffled. The dust and the stale air choked my nostrils. I looked at every face as we sat on sacks of corn Father hid down there. William, with his blond hair and wide-set eyes, looked the spitting image of Father, trying to keep a straight face with all his might. But at age seven, it looked more like he was holding his breath. Little Mary, two years younger, played with the rag doll Mrs. Bush gave her. She was far away from any of us in her pretend world. I wished I could be there too. Robert, just three, leaned on Mama with a look of absolute misery on his face. Mama looked a little wide eyed and frightened, almost far away as she held baby John and suckled him. Looking at my family, all my pride at being a loyal Confederate got mighty thin. It wasn't in my people's blood to belong, though I wanted to belong so fiercely. We were outcasts nearly everywhere. Why pretend it wasn't true? It wasn't in my blood to belong, not to the Confederacy, not to any world.

Mama's lantern flickered as Mrs. Shelburn backed down the ladder. At the bottom she wiped her hands like she always did at the end of a chore. "Shooting's getting worse, sister Mary. It may come this way." Why didn't her words frighten me anymore? I was so weary of everything, of not knowing what to believe in or who to believe in anymore. I wanted to crawl up with little Robert and lean on Mama. But Mama looked as bewildered as I felt. I reckon I saw then what, without the war I would have seen far later in life: my mama was just a woman. She didn't have no magic answers for the problems that faced us. She just said a prayer and threw her best answer at the problem. She looked almost like me.

I'm not sure just what gave me the confidence to do what I did next, but I got up and sat next to Mama and hugged her. It wasn't a taking hug; it was a giving hug. I don't know how you tell the difference, but she knew. Yet, I felt so terribly alone. Was it alone-ness? No. It was more like I'd been shoved in front of everybody to walk first on a path through the dark. And I didn't want to walk it. I wanted to run away to Mr. Rochester and Thornfield Hall. But what I got was standing out on my own in the middle of this war, feeling everything and feeling nothing at the same time. I got all grown up in that cellar, like it or not, in the space of an hour and here I was still thirteen years old.

Mrs. Shelburn got up after an hour or two and climbed the ladder. We all got real quiet. When she came down she solemnly announced, "They've stopped, thanks be to God." When she said that, I got up and went up the ladder first. Mrs. Shelburn and Mama looked at me speechless, but there must have been something in my eyes and they just let me. Maybe they could see what I was feeling.

The kitchen and the parlor were both real quiet. I went out the back door and all I could hear was the birds singing their old songs. I left the door to the house open and walked down to where the road passes our farm. It seemed quiet, just like any other First Day. Then the breeze came up and I smelled it, from the west. It smelled of sulfur and burning fume and the rank smell I remembered from the time when we found one of Father's cows dead after a while, all flyblown and rotting. The rotting smell was sickening. I turned and went in the house again as the sky darkened up and threatened to rain.

The smell was still there when William and I walked to school in the chilly, cloudy morning. I was filled with a low dread the likes I had not known since Father was arrested. But this time the thoughts of my schoolmates seemed a small thing next to the dark, evil smelling thing to the west. William and I walked mighty slow. As we got closer to the school the smell grew stronger still. About halfway I saw Josiah standing at the edge of the road, looking down at something just off to the right.

We came up to him and he looked up at us. There were tears in his eyes and the books hung limply in their strap from his right hand. I looked where he looked and the shock made me reel. The rotting smell came up and slapped me in the face. In the ditch lay a young soldier in grey. His left leg was clean gone, as if it had never been there. His unmoving eyes stared up in the rustling branches over his head and he lay back almost casually, as if just taking in the beauty of that cold morning.

I think I said, "Oh, my Jesus," and I don't know for how long we all stood looking. But then without thinking about it, I clutched Josiah's free hand and commanded, "Come on. You've got to leave this." William must have been aghast to hear me talk with the sinful 'you', but I wasn't thinking of that. With all my strength I intended to drag Josiah Clark away from that corpse if I had to. Thank God, he didn't fight me much. We came away up the road with me pulling William from my left hand and Josiah from my right, right into the school yard and through the school house door where Miss Emily wasn't standing as usual.

We found her inside at her desk, leaning her chin on her clasped hands. The other students sat silently and I was sure that we were not the only ones to see evidence of the battle on the way in. When Josiah and William had sat down on the boys side and I'd sat down amongst the girls, Miss Emily got up in front, still looking at the floor, and in a voice of much agitation said, "Let us bow our heads a moment in silent prayer for those men who gave their lives for their country yesterday." We all bowed and I did pray for all the boys lying in the woods and fields that day. And I prayed my Josiah wouldn't be like them. When we raised our heads again, Miss Emily took a breath to steady herself and launched into the lesson for the day.

I dreaded the moment it came time for us to walk home. I had no more faith in my plan to become regular folks. How was I to tell Josiah that? But I didn't try to run away. When it came time to leave he waited for me at the door as usual. I made up my mind to say as little as possible. No reason to just blurt it out. As we walked on, I found I hadn't any reason to worry. Josiah watched the ground and said nothing. His eyes frightened me: they were shocked and far away. Finally, when we got to the road junction where we parted each day, he said very softly, "Maggie, you must remember your promise to remember me when I'm gone."

"I promise," I whispered back, and then I kissed him on the cheek for the second time and walked on toward home. He was never to walk me home again.

Arriving at school the next day, things seemed more back to normal. The first couple of hours went by uneventfully. I was at Thornfield Hall when a fire broke out and Mr. Rochester was rushing upstairs to save the madwoman in the attic. Then we heard the popping like rocks against a wall. Miss Emily stopped her lesson for a moment to listen. We all listened. It was coming from the west and it seemed to be coming closer. We heard the boom of cannon like a blow to our faces. Josiah became lively, saying, "Miss Emily. Maybe all the little children best go home." His eyes glowed with a fear that I'd never seen in them before.

"No, Josiah. I think we're all much safer in here. I'd worry more to have you children wandering outside. Perhaps it won't get any closer. Let's try and go on with the lesson." I tried to go back to the fire at Thornfield Hall, but the popping got closer still. The other children got restless.

"Settle down, children," Miss Emily said, without much conviction in her voice. I think this made us all more frightened than ever.

Just then an explosion rocked us and the schoolhouse creaked. We all screamed, even some of the boys I think. The sound of rifle fire got real loud, so we could hear it clearly.

"Please, Miss Emily," Josiah shouted over the din, "the children won't be safe here!"

She seemed dazed, but she rapidly ordered, "All you children who live to the west, go home with someone who lives to the east." And she began pairing us off. The Coulter children, Ray and Ida, were to go with William and me. Josiah moved around the room, reassuring the children and hurrying them out the door. Everybody left their school books and slates behind, but I grabbed *Jane Eyre*. Miss Emily and Josiah left last.

Outside the noise of battle was deafening. We heard shells whining overhead before they exploded terrifically loud. We got maybe a hundred yards before another whining shell got louder and louder.

"Get down!" Josiah screamed, shoving Miss Emily and me off our feet. We all fell into the leaves like books tipping each over on a shelf when the bookend is pulled, and good thing too. For our log schoolhouse exploded into a million flying splinters that whistled over our heads.

VI
Farewell Forever

I don't know that we'd have gotten home except that I took William, Ray and Ida through my shortcut over Mr. Crabtree's place and so got us all off the road. The battle was coming down the road and even as we ran, grey soldiers galloped past us toward Jonesville. The Yankees must have been winning this one, though I didn't see any right then.

When we got home Mrs. Shelburn was outside looking for us, her eyes wide open with fear I'd never seen before. She hurried us down the ladder into the cellar. Down below we could hear the battle clearly this time. The sound of gunfire was close and every once in a while we heard something crash and shatter upstairs. Ray and Ida looked mighty scared, as did my brothers and sisters. Little Mary and Robert hid their faces in Mama's skirt. It got louder and louder and then almost as fast it got softer and softer. I couldn't stand it anymore. I rushed up the ladder and into our house before Mrs. Shelburn or Mama could holler. Two windows were shot out, and some dishes were smashed on the floor. One wall was pocked with bullet holes that let the sun in like tiny windows, but beyond that there wasn't much damage. The air smelled singed with the stinging reek of gunpowder. The calendar by the back door had been shot away and was swinging loose. I'll always remember the page with the date flapping loosely in the cold breeze from the shattered window: December 1, 1863.

Mama was up the ladder right behind me. "Maggie!" she whispered loudly, hoarseness in her voice.

"It's all right, Mama. They're gone." Father would have dragged me back just on the principle of obedience. Mama thought about it and stepped up into the room with me. Then she rushed to my side when I sucked in my breath.

Out the shattered window that looked up our driveway to the road I plainly saw horseback soldiers and wagons riding east to Jonesville. The soldiers were too far to see clearly but there was no mistaking that they all wore blue uniforms. Back up the road a piece, about where the Clark farm should be, there was a column of thick black smoke. I thought of Josiah, and Father and all the men we knew. Please Lord Jesus, no. Don't let them be dead.

Words came to Mama, "Oh thanks be to God! They've come at last!" Then she saw the smoke and gasped, "Oh, my Henry!"

My heart tumbled in my breast. I wanted to be angry with her, with all of us, for being such traitors to our country, but then, I understood what it meant to her. If Lee County fell under Union occupation, then for us at least, the war would be over. Joel could come back. Father might come home safely. We'd be in touch again with the meetings of Friends in the north. Maybe even we could go north ourselves and move in amongst the Friends. Everything she wanted depended on the soldiers in blue. My mother was a traitor to our country and I couldn't blame her for wanting it. Or maybe she was loyal to the old country. I hadn't thought of it that way before. What could I do or say? I fell to straightening out the kitchen just to have something to do.

It was at least two days before we ventured off of the farm again, though Mrs. Shelburn took Ray and Ida home in the wagon. We lived quietly, working in the garden and eating small meals. I went to bed early each night with a long candle and lost myself in *Jane Eyre*. Jane had discovered Mr. Rochester's mad wife and had fled into the moor. I quieted my heart when I read that; I felt like running too, but there was no place to go.

During all the second day, soldiers in blue rode west along our road, back from Jonesville and out to the Gap where they come from. Mama was disappointed, I could tell. I couldn't say how I felt, such a fog come over my heart. Late afternoon on the third day, Minerva Bush came across the cold, dusty road with a basket under her arm and excitement written over her face. We could feel she had news before she reached the door. When Mama invited her in she looked around at the bullet holes and the windows Mrs. Shelburn had boarded up. Minerva Bush was a tall, thin woman of past forty years, with small, squinty eyes and iron grey hair invading the last of her brown hair. Her coat and dress were severely worn; she seemed to have been through a lot. Mama found some tea to offer her and we all sat down around the kitchen table to hear her news.

"Mary Milbourn and Mary Shelburn," she said, enjoying herself, "I have so much to tell thee both."

"Well, tell us then, sister," Mrs. Shelburn interrupted brusquely.

Mrs. Bush paused long enough to lick her lips and let out a little smile like a cat does when he's caught a mouse. "Well, thy husbands are both well, as is my John. The regiment was badly beaten in that wicked fighting. They've set up what's left of their camp at Hickory Flat."

"East of Jonesville?" Mama gasped.

"Yes, sister. They lost most everything too. The Yankees destroyed their camp and the Clark farm. It's the judgment of God upon their violent ways."

I stopped breathing for a moment. Mrs. Bush continued, "Jemima Clark and her boy got away, but they don't own a thing on God's earth now. The Yankees burned their farm to the ground. They're staying with the Penningtons. Marilyn is Jemima's sister's daughter, you know."

She said much more that had to do with other farms affected by the battle, and about her Tom in Indiana, but I didn't hear any more. I thought of Josiah, devastated by the battle right on his home. I yearned to see Josiah, but I was surely not welcome at the Pennington farm. But sometimes, it's funny, we actually get the things we wish for. Mrs. Bush left us when the gossip was exhausted. I felt a weariness like I'd never felt before. After our meager supper of cornmeal cakes and milk, I said I was feeling poorly, excused myself and went to bed even earlier than usual with my candles.

In my book, Jane had found a home with her cousins and a new life, leaving poor Mr. Rochester behind. I couldn't help but feel that Jane was a might too cruel on poor Mr. Rochester. Darkness grew outside my window and I lit my candle. Sometimes I get to pondering for a long time. I love to stare out my window and let my thoughts wander, to think everything over without no brothers or sister interrupting me for hours maybe. I watched the light go from grey to blood orange to purple to deep blue, then black. Night was a lovely thing, with stars and the moon all over the sky. It was easy to pretend you were in another place where they didn't fight and there weren't no Friends and Regular Folk; everyone in that world were just folks and there weren't no dividing lines at all.

All of a sudden a dark shape blocked out the stars and I realized that a man was looking in my window. A chill of fright pulsed through me and I think

I was going to scream when he pressed his face against the window. Lord have mercy; it was Josiah.

"Maggie!" he whispered loudly. I could see his head and shoulders framed clearly, hanging onto the tree branch outside my window. I jumped off the bed, unmindful of the fact I only had my nightgown on, and rushed to the window, throwing it up and leaning on the sill.

"Josiah!" I whispered, "What are you doing here?" I was used to talking like regular folks with him now, but I feared I gave him the idea I didn't want to see him. "I'm sorry 'bout your farm," I added.

"I wanted to see you, Maggie, 'fore I left."

"Where you goin'?" I think my heart stopped.

"I'm going to join Pa with Gen'l Lee. Ma doesn't want me to go but I'm near sixteen. My cousin, Ralph, he's a month older than me and he's already in Gen'l Lee's army."

I couldn't think of a word to say to save my life.

Josiah sensed this and said, "Well, I just wanted to tell you, 'cause you promised…to remember me."

"Oh, yes, I will, Josiah, always."

He looked at me what seemed like hours, then kissed me lightly on the lips, almost falling out of the tree to do so. "I'll always remember thee, Maggie Milbourn." Then he was gone into the night. I last saw his shadow running, black against the silent stars. After a time I closed the window, blew out my candle and lay in the dark, sleepless, almost all night long.

I think any hope I had up to that point left me that night. I moved through the day's chores wordlessly. The world became for me one long, grey passage marked with sunrises and sunsets. Mama grew concerned for me, I could tell; but what could she do. Our lives were a constant struggle just to keep from being hungry: cooking and cleaning and feeding the children. Even with the cold weather, Mrs. Shelburn got spring vegetable seed into the garden. I did a lot of the hoeing. Work felt good, and helped the dull ache in my soul a little. Though I didn't feel it at the time, I was treated like a third adult and there was a bit of comfort in that. Nobody nagged or scolded me; if I didn't pull my weight, somebody went to bed hungry, so pull I did. I found that's what it really means to be grown up: to do things not because somebody told you, but because everything depends on you.

I got the most comfort from my book. Jane too was near despair. Her life with her cousins had been fine until her cousin, a man called St.John, as cold a heart as ever lived, began to pester her about marrying him, making it out to be God's will. How could he know? How did anyone know? The Yankees thought it God's will to conquer our state. Our boys thought it God's will to protect it. And together they laid each other in the grave and reduced my family and my soul to dust. Worse than all of that, they took my Josiah. I had a hard time praying at night, but I always did beg for the life of my Josiah.

In fact I was trying to pray in my room one night about four days after the battle when I heard a lot of dishes clattering, cupboard doors slamming and low voices downstairs in the kitchen. Lord, soldiers must be coming, I thought. I got up, put on a wrap, opened my door, and clattered downstairs. My father sat at the kitchen table, or at least a man who looked like my father. He was thin and gaunt, his clothes torn and dirt laced. He slumped on his chair like a rag. Mama and Mrs. Shelburn were hustling to fix up something on the stove. Father looked at me and said my name, "Maggie," in a voice just above a whisper.

Yes, I know I was supposed to be mad at him, but somehow I just ran over there and wrapped my arms around his neck the way he used to let me when I was just a very little girl. He didn't stop me neither and if I was mad at him, I just forgot it. "Papa," I whispered. Then I felt foolish. I had never called him 'papa' in all my thirteen years. He wouldn't have liked it. I expected him to stiffen up like he always did. But after a moment, he put up his thin, weathered hand and touched my arm. He did, he touched my arm, like somebody else might. I was gloriously happy for that touch. But Mama and Mrs. Shelburn clacked the plates of food on the table and the moment ended. Life's like that; you finally reach the moment you've hoped for and it lasts 'bout as long as a sneeze. Still, you got to be grateful; it wouldn't be no good any other way.

"Sit thee down, Maggie," Mama dictated in a hurried voice. Then she sat down on the other side of Papa while he ate. "Eat slowly, Henry, or thee'll be sick. Tell us what happened." Mrs. Shelburn sat down across the table and folded her hands in concern. Papa swallowed a mouthful of cornbread and looking down into his food, told his story.

"After the Yankees run off the soldiers, they took us out to Hickory Flat. The Yankees destroyed most of the food and lots of fellers were sick from rotten beef. There wasn't enough of even that to go around. George and Dick and I wouldn't eat no more of it. We got hungry and weak, till they didn't even set a guard over us. Told us they figured we'd be dead in the morning and good riddance to yellow bellied Quakers. George and I got to crawling, seeing as there was no guard. The others followed. When we got clear, I told everyone we had to walk in the dark. Walking was so hard, so hard. Didn't think I'd live to see thee, the pain was so bad. We waited till nightfall, resting and then we stood up and walked through Jonesville as far as the Bush place. Thy husband, Mary Shelburn, had to be helped, but he's there."

Mrs. Shelburn got up, "I must go to him."

Mama said, "We've got to get them all to the Yankees at the Gap. Thee knows it, Henry. Thy stubborn pride will only get thee hanged if thee stays."

Papa nodded and Mrs. Shelburn slipped quietly out the door saying only, "I will be back." Mama wrapped her arms around his shoulders. He kept eating like the food was holy. When he paused for a bit, he said, "I'm sorry, Mary, to put thee through this. Thee was right. I shoulda went with Joel and Tom." Mama said nothing but I was truly amazed. I'd never heard my father apologize for anything in his life. Then he looked up at me and for a moment there was a flicker of that thing I'd seen in his eyes that first time we visited him in the guard house, that loving need for me. But he put his eyes back down to his plate and continued eating. Oh, but for me it was enough, just enough. My heart was clear. I was no daughter of the Confederacy. Let the Yankees come. Three cheers for Union.

Father stopped eating and shook his head when Mama offered him more. And suddenly, just as I found my father, I realized I was going to lose him. Mama said it first. "Thee must go now, Henry, while it is still dark."

"I can't walk to the Gap, Mary."

"Take Old Pet."

"But thee needs him, and the children."

"We'll manage. Come on. Now."

And my mama became forceful, gently pulling Father from his chair, dressing him in fresh clothes, packing him a food bag, and leading him outside to the barn. She saddled Old Pet who was just as sleepy day or night.

"They'll come looking for me," he said, "They'll know thee had a horse."

"I'll tell them bushwhackers stole him, or Yankees." She gave Father the food bag, and shoved him up the side of Old Pet. But Father was too weak to mount. Mama threw up her hands in frustration and anguish.

"Wait!" I cried, and I led Old Pet to the box I used to get up on his back.

"That's my girl!" Mama laughed, delighted. Together we helped haul Father up on Old Pet's back where he took the reins and slumped in the saddle.

"God go with thee, Henry my love," Mama said, squeezing his hand. "When thee reaches brother George, send us word if thee can. Stay off the roads; go across the fields. And kick Old Pet. Thee must get far away before daylight comes."

Father reached down and caressed her cheek with what little strength he had. Then he looked at me with that treasured look once again. I held his hand and he let me for a moment. Then he clicked his tongue and Old Pet moved out of the barn. Father's hand slowly slid from mine. I watched him go, wiping my eyes. He headed into the cloudy night, west across Crabtree's fields and away from the roads. I watched him until he vanished in the darkness.

When I turned around, Mama was pounding at the barn door hinges with a hammer. "Help me," she ordered. I found another hammer, a smaller one, and started to pounding the hinges on the other side. Within a few minutes, we had shattered both hinges. Then pulling together, we ripped the barn doors off so that they collapsed to the ground with a large slap. Mama stood back, breathing hard, clapping the dust off her hands. "There," she said, "That's what bushwhackers did to get at our horse." I laughed. But Mama said, "Hush now, and remember that was bushwhackers. We're sure to have woken the children. Come, let's go in." Some thrill went through me when she didn't include me with the other children. I'd never felt so grown up.

But if I enjoyed that feeling, it wasn't for long. Mrs. Shelburn returned in the early morning hours bearing the news that her husband and the others were off for the Gap too. She also heard that General Longstreet had failed to take Knoxville and was on the run from the armies of the Yankee General Grant. It was stunning news. We knew like a bell had rung, that the Confederacy was lost and we rejoiced. We slept in joy only to be woken up at daybreak, a few short hours later. Captain Garson and two bedraggled cavalrymen sat on their horses in our yard. Oh, please Jesus, merciful Jesus, no. Mama and Mrs. Shelburn were out talking to them. I put on a wrap over my nightgown and went to the door to hear them talking.

"...they've been gone about a day. We figure they came here."

"They aren't here," Mama said. I noticed how carefully she skirted around the outright lie. "We had bushwhackers come this way, though. You can see what happened to our barn..."

Captain Garson cut her off impatiently. "Just the same, ma'am, we intend to search the house."

"Will thee and thy men want some breakfast?" Mrs. Shelburn offered and I quietly gasped. Captain Garson and the men were moving to dismount and you could see for just a moment his surprise at the offer.

"Much obliged, ma'am," he replied. They dismounted, tied off their horses and all started into the house. Mama spotted me and commanded, "Go wake thy brothers and sisters, Maggie." I turned and ran inside in fright.

VII
The Coming of Thunder

How could Mrs. Shelburn just invite them in to interrogate me? Didn't she realize what she was risking? It was one thing to let them look around, another to stare them in the face for the length of breakfast and not tell them where Papa was. I was furious with her, but I didn't have no time to think about it. I wasn't sure I could face Captain Garson and hide the fact that my father no doubt was still just a few miles away, trying to make the Cumberland Gap and the Yankee lines on a horse that moved slower than molasses in January. And these men with their swift horses could catch him up in less than two hour's time. Everything depended on what I said and if I could keep up a straight face. Lord Jesus help me!

One thing for sure was that shy Maggie Milbourn was sure to get asked what she'd seen and she would start to cry and tell that her papa was just lately gone. Captain Garson would ride out and her papa would hang for sure as a deserter, all because she was shy Maggie Milbourn. Suddenly I loathed and despised that side of myself. I wanted to kill it dead. Maybe I did, too. I went upstairs into the children's room and roused them all with the words, "Soldiers are here", then dashed through the connecting door to my room, slipped on my black school dress and brushed out my hair. I was sorry I didn't have a chance to wash up at the pump outside, but there was nothing I could do about that.

When I opened my door, went downstairs and emerged in the kitchen, I was a young lady of grace. I pretended I was Miss Emily and walked with her poise. Captain Garson and his two men were sitting around the table absorbed in eating cornbread and potatoes. It wasn't much of a meal but they seemed ready enough for any food. Mama and Mrs. Shelburn kept themselves busy serving. When I came in I could see on Captain Garson's face that he saw me as a southern lady. I sat down and started making talk, hoping to take the talk for as long as possible away from the thing I didn't want to talk about.

"Good morning, Captain. It's so very good to see thee. How's Miss Emily? I miss seeing her so." All this sounded odd coming out of my mouth with the combination of southern belle and Quaker 'thee.' But Captain Garson seemed quite surprised by my manner. He hesitated a moment before answering.

"Thank you for asking. Miss Emily is well, but as you may guess, she is quite upset by the battle and what happened to the schoolhouse. I will tell her you asked after her."

And then there came an awkward silence around the table. If Captain Garson meant to take the tone of the constable and question us, he seemed to have lost the will. I decided to be like a soldier myself; I had blunted Captain Garson's charge with my politeness, now I had to press my advantage. Words came out of my mouth like a runaway train.

"I'm sorry that our breakfast is so little. There isn't much food left on the farm these days. I remember when we used to have feasts before the war"...In mid sentence an idea came to me and I launched recklessly into it without much thought. "...But that was before Papa was in the army and we had horses here. Why just this week our last horse was stolen..." Then the boldest stroke of all came out of my mouth. It wasn't quite a lie I guess but I don't recall thinking about it before I heard my mouth say it. "How is my Papa these days?"

Captain Garson looked up at me in disbelief, which only made my tongue wag even more. I began to dread that I had really made a mistake now, but I kept talking like an old magpie about the horse, hoping to change the subject I had brought up. "That ol' horse really was a poor one. Couldn't get but one walk out of him and that one was mighty slow. Who does thee think would want to rip our barn doors off for a worthless horse like that, Captain?" I paused, simply out of breath and feeling foolish. Now I'd done it for sure. I was ready to run from the room in tears but the Maggie in me that wasn't shy just smiled at Captain Garson and tasted her cornbread while the shy Maggie in me just watched myself in amazement.

"I reckon I don't know, miss." He turned from me and faced Mama over his shoulder. "Now, if you don't mind ma'am, my men and I will search the house."

Of course, mind or not, we all knew they would search. Mama nodded at the courtesy and the three men got up, screeching their chairs across the kitchen floor. They clumped upstairs and down like giants with big boots. Fortunately, all the little ones had leaked into the kitchen while I was gabbing, so the rooms were empty. Still, I dreaded the direct question about Papa. Would Mama lie and commit a sin or tell the truth and hang her husband? I looked at her and she must have reflected the nervousness in my own face. And suddenly I knew she couldn't lie to them; she loved truth so much she couldn't bend it like that. It was one thing for her to pull the barn doors off and hope they distracted the soldiers but put to a direct question she would tell the truth no matter what.

And then my legs were moving upstairs. For some reason I was convinced I was going to die and nothing mattered anymore. I was the sacrifice. I found Captain Garson and his men pounding on floorboards with their heals and on walls with their fists. What were they doing? They it occurred to me they were sounding for hidden doors. My mouth said, "Captain, sir." How un-Quaker to call anyone 'sir', but this was the not-shy Maggie that had taken over me. "Thee didn't say a word about my Papa. Was he killed in the battle?" And then I knew I had to cry for him. I knew it couldn't be overdone or they would know it was made up. So I buried my face in my hands against the doorpost and squeezed my eyes till they hurt and watered, and I didn't turn around again until Captain Garson spoke.

"Well, miss, no. He wasn't killed in the battle, exactly. Uh, well I'm sorry to report, Miss Maggie, but your father has deserted."

I stood there and let my mouth hang open a little. Then I ran to the kitchen table and sat, putting my head down. It was the best I could do. Mama and Mrs. Shelburn stood by the wash basin, their faces tight like skins on a drum. My heart felt like it was in a vice. Down the hall I heard Capt. Garson cuss some and then he said, "C'mon sergeant, mount up. He ain't here."

"But Cap'n, he's been here and..."

"Shut up and mount, sergeant!"

"Yessir."

I heard their boots clumping down the stairs. Capt. Garson led them across the kitchen and stopped to face Mama. All was lost, I just knew it.

"We'll be leaving you now, ma'am. Thank you kindly for breakfast." And they walked out the back door. Oh, but they knew. We hadn't fooled them in the least. Still, surely Captain Garson knew that we knew when Papa had left and which way he was going. Why didn't he question us? Could it be that he really believed my acting? I got up and rushed to a window on the north side of the house where he and his men mounted their horses. I made sure I couldn't be seen. Captain Garson got up and looked around at our house with a look on his face I couldn't quite read. Was it disgust that I would try to fool him? Or was it chagrin for having upset such a 'lady' as me? He clicked his tongue and his horse broke into a trot, followed by the two cavalrymen. When they reached the road, the turned west and vanished in the trees. A cold chill raced down my back. What did it matter that he didn't question us? He would catch Papa anyway. Still, if my acting had saved Mama having to betray her husband, it was worth it.

And suddenly I knew they were going to hang my father, sure as I stood there. And I hated that war and everybody who was responsible for all the dead bodies of our loved ones, on both sides and caught in the middle. I wished for some kind of magic that would just make them stop. Stop! Stop! Don't hang my Papa. Not for states' rights or national pride, or union. Stop! Stop! If there'd been someone there to scream at, I would have.

I took to praying a lot, but God seemed to have run off. And when I thought about it, I guess I didn't know what I believed, or if I believed anything at all. No God stopped them from hanging my Papa.

I don't rightly remember much that happened for a while after this. Captain Garson came on Seventh Day. We were all too ill to have Meeting on First Day next. I suppose we ate meals, slept and fed the cow, but I can't recall it. I do remember the little ones playing, and I remember trying to read *Jane Eyre*, but it wasn't no good. When I got to the part where Mr. Rochester was wounded, hid the book and didn't take it out any more. I didn't want to know what happened next. I trudged through the grey passage that was greyer still for Papa's death, and positively black too without believing in the Lord. I didn't believe in nothing but war and dying sooner or later. I think at least a week went by. Can't say for sure. I felt no emotion for more than a week. The only thing I recall is that we had our first light snow on the mountain.

Then on the next First Day the road began to rumble with the thunder of hooves. Mama and Mrs. Shelburn rushed to the window and Mama let out a little scream. I followed slowly. Soldiers in blue were streaming east down the Jonesville road. Lord knows why, but I suddenly found myself running down the drive up to the road in the chill air. I stopped at our gate and stared in wonder at the boys in smart blue uniforms riding by on horseback in columns of two, their shiny sabers rattling against the flanks of their well fed mounts. How different this looked from the lean, ill-dressed men and the thin horses of the 64th Virginia. Three small cannons rolled by, drawn by their caissons and teams of horses. Men shouted to the team horses. And all this time, something like morning was growing in my dark heart. I stood in the road and waved, "Please stop and talk to me!" A rider with a dark beard pulled out of the column, followed by a younger, beardless man with curly red hair, real handsome too. The first rider stopped and touched the brim of his blue kepi with his fingers.

"Ma'am."

"Please, has thee seen my Papa? He was riding for the Gap 'bout a week and a half ago."

The bearded soldier thought a moment and shook his head, but the red-headed soldier spoke first, "Sorry, miss. Lot's of fellows make it to the Gap and we send them on. What's your name, little lady?"

I'm sure I must have been sagging in black disappointment, but I managed to answer him, "Maggie Milbourn."

"Well, I'm Corporal O'Keefe and this is Sergeant Llewellyn, 16th Illinois. Pleased to meet you. This your farm?"

"Yes."

"You Quakers, huh? The rebs go after your papa?"

I nodded mournfully.

"Sure sorry, little lady. He could've made it, you know. Lots of fellows come through. You seen the rebs around here lately?"

"They came looking for Papa last week."

"Are they up in Jonesville?"

I shrugged. I didn't know.

"Well," Sergeant Llewellyn grumbled, "if they're sending out conscriptors, they can't be far. Say, little lady. Your papa don't own a mill hereabouts, does he?"

"Surely, he does."

The two soldiers looked at each other and smiled. Corporal O'Keefe asked, "Do you reckon he'd mind if some of our boys ground some corn there?"

"No," I replied, thinking that Papa would have gladly given food to the boys in blue; anything but fighting. "I reckon he wouldn't mind."

"Thank you, little lady," said Sergeant Llewellyn, "We'll be back." And they spurred their horses into a gallop and were gone in a cloud of dust up the road.

We were too far away to hear gunfire this time, but just the same, we were in a state of agitation all that day. So when next morning, the sound of boots pounded the front porch and a fist banged on the door, my heart leaped into my mouth. Confederates or Yankees? I answered the door. There stood Corporal O'Keefe and Sergeant Llewellyn, covered with dirt and smiling like they were on a First Day visit. Beside them stood a tall, bearded officer in a blue, double breasted coat with epaulets on his shoulders and a golden belt around his waist, from which hung a saber. Corporal O'Keefe touched the brim of his kepi, "Afternoon, Miss Milbourn. You remember us, I hope. This is Major Beeres. Could we come in?"

I couldn't think of anything to say. The bold Maggie had risen in my anger the day Captain Garson came, but here I found no anger. These men would have saved Papa's life if they could have. I led them into the entry way and Mama and Mrs. Shelburn came out. Mama smiled like she hadn't in a long time. Major Beeres took off his hat and introduced himself.

"Thee is welcome here," Mama replied, "I have little to offer, but thee and thy men are welcome at our table."

"Thank you kindly," the major replied and followed Mama into the kitchen. We were fat that day. Mama had a little of one of Minerva Bush's chickens to add to the cornbread this time. It seemed a feast; in fact, by this time I couldn't remember what a big meal was like. The Major was very polite, thanking Mama for everything put before him and making small talk. Some of his people had been Friends and he was familiar with our ways. Of course Mama asked him if he remembered Papa coming through the Gap.

"Sorry, Mrs. Milbourn, I can't really say. Several Friends came through couple of weeks ago, but Colonel Lemert's regiment was on duty and I didn't pay any mind at the time to the names of those who got through."

Mama sagged a little and her eyes went down to her plate, though she didn't eat. I knew what she felt; I felt it too. She was a widow, sure. The major let the silence alone for a moment then said, "What we came to ask, Mrs. Milbourn, is if my men could use your husband's mill to grind some of the corn we've requisitioned hereabouts."

"Certainly," she replied, "Maggie can show thy men where it is."

The men rose from the table, their chairs screeching on the wood floor. When I followed them outside to where their horses were tied up it came home to me that I had no way to ride with them. I'd almost forgot that Papa took Old Pet. Corporal O'Keefe looked at me quizzically, "What's the matter, Miss Milbourn?"

"We don't have no horses anymore. Papa took our last one to get to the Gap."

He smiled the most beautiful smile I ever did see on a man. "Come on up and ride with me."

I hesitated and looked back at Mama in the doorway. She shrugged as if to say she guessed it would be all right. Corporal O'Keefe hung down his left hand. I grasped it and he pulled my weight up like it was nothing. Lord, I felt mighty shy sitting that close behind him on the saddle. But the horse was big and strong, a beautiful buckskin with black feet, mane and tail. We walked on, following the major and Sergeant Llewellyn. Corporal O'Keefe's saber clanked lightly against my left leg at every step. A cold wind cut through me and I leaned closer to the corporal for warmth.

"What was your name again?" he asked.

"Maggie."

"Well, Maggie, I'm Connor and you're sitting on Willie."

"He's beautiful," I ventured to say. When we reached the road I pointed to the west, up to Long Hollow Road and we all turned that way. The road was rutted dry mud by this time of the year and the wind off Cumberland Mountain smelled of snow.

"How old are you?" Connor asked.

"Thirteen, almost fourteen."

"That's how old my little sister is. Her name's Mary. She lives with my Mama and Papa up in Galesburg." He paused. "I haven't seen her in near two years." He told me all about his family and they sounded like nice folks.

About this time we were passing the Crabtree place and there were tents and more soldiers in blue all over. Cooking fires left tall trails of smoke into the midday sky. We passed by the road to Crabtree's, where Major Beeres and Sergeant Llewellyn ordered Connor to take a squad up to Papa's mill. They rode down the lane to Crabtree's place and shortly after, seven Yankees on horseback came up and fell in with Connor.

We rode up past the gate to Papa's north pasture before I spotted the line of men trudging up the road ahead of us dressed in butternut and grey. We caught up with them pretty quick. I counted twenty-six. I could see they were tied together with their wrists behind them and four mounted soldiers in blue watched them closely. They were headed for the Gap and prison sure. I didn't want to look at their faces but I couldn't help it. They were all strangers, thank God, until I saw the first prisoner in line. I didn't recognize him at first without his hat and with the blood and bandages over the right side of his face and on his right shoulder. But the piercing anger in his stare almost melted me down. It was Captain Garson.

VIII
The Troubled Waters of Friendship

I'm sure I hid my face in Connor's back. I didn't want to see. Lord, what must he think of me, sitting up with a Yankee on a horse. But then, how was he ever a friend to me? He was mighty polite when we went to visit Papa, and I reckon I'll never know what pull my acting had with him the day he came to look for Papa. He was engaged to Miss Emily. He had no more claim on me than that. He might have treated me like a lady, but he dragged my Papa into the army and stripped our farm of food. I looked back at him, now far behind. His gaze turned toward the dirt in front of him. I reckon he didn't think that much of me. He'd led my Papa away trussed up like a hog; now it was his turn. This is war, ain't no real fairness to it; it's just that nobody has good luck for too long, that's all, nobody. But I resolved, first chance I got, I'd go see Miss Emily and tell her he wasn't dead. I could do that much for her.

Little further down the road we turned right up into Long Hollow proper the way I used to go to school. After some time we passed what was left of the schoolhouse. I hadn't seen it since I fled that day. It was thoroughly destroyed, just a heap of shattered logs. My heart started to feel so full that it was about to explode and I wanted to scream or cry; I didn't even know why. But I held it in. Who was there to tell anyway?

About that time we came up to Papa's mill by the side of Long Hollow Run. Just then a bleak sun broke through the cloud cover, as if trying to remind us it was morning. Connor handed me down off Willie and he and his squad dismounted, tying off their horses to the trees on the land. The door hadn't been opened since early last fall and we had a time getting it to swing to. But with all them Yankees to heave on it, it finally gave way. A wagon pulled up behind the horses, stacked with sacks of corn. Connor's squad lost no time in opening up the sluice gate that let the water down over the wheel and set the stones turning. Papa had imported special grinding stones from France and I could tell the Yankees were impressed. But for me, the sounds of those old stones whirring together brought back all the memories of Papa working here in peaceful times, when our neighbors regarded us with friendship and not scorn. Something in me burst and I fled out the back door, down to the edge of the creek and had me the first good cry since they hung Papa. I had been at it but a short time when I heard Connor speak behind me, "What's the matter, Maggie?"

I looked at him. Here was this gentle Yankee, whom not too long ago I wanted to see dead as I wanted to see all Yankees dead. And here he was, just like he was home in Galesburg, talking to his sister Mary. I hesitated. Then he asked me about my people, about Grandfather and Uncle Joel, and made me tell him the whole story of how Papa escaped the 64th Virginia.

"I'll tell you what," he said when I finished, "When I go back to camp, I'll find out who was on duty that day at the first checkpoint and see if I can find out if your pa went through."

A mist of hope rose in my heart. I needed to talk to someone. Dare I trust this Yankee. My heart made the decision without waiting for my head. "Oh Connor, I am so confused. I saw a man I know in those Confederate prisoners. He was the one who took my Papa off, maybe hung him, but he's also engaged to my teacher. And now he's a prisoner. And that heap of logs we passed, that was my school. We was almost killed in it." I was shaking, but the words kept tumbling out. "And I seen a dead soldier, and he was just a boy. And a boy I know, he gone off to fight for General Lee. Then I was listening to them old millstones and it set me to thinking about Papa before the war. I hate this war! I just hate it. It ain't fair. It just ain't fair at all. I don't know who to trust or what to think. I just don't understand it. And I don't think no God would allow such a thing if he was up there."

There was a long pause. My heart felt empty, like everything come out of it. Connor sat in the grass and chewed a stem of grass. "Well," he said, thinking, "I reckon you're right about the war. I suppose if I were you, I wouldn't know who to trust either. I'm sorry someone as young as you has to be so troubled." He thought about this a while, then added, "But I ain't given up on God yet, Maggie. I figure maybe God lets us do whatever we want down here. Some men do bad things, try and break up our country. I wanted to help stop that. But I don't much care for fighting just to fight.

"When this war's over and we've licked the Rebs, I'm going back to Galesburg and take over my daddy's store, marry Fiona Sullivan and have children. And I ain't gonna think about this time much, if I can help it."

"What's she like?" I asked.

"Fiona? Ah, she's a grand girl. Hair as black as night, and the prettiest face." Then he stopped and was lost in thought.

A Yankee called from the mill, "Corpr'l?"

Connor got up. "'Scuse me," he said and walked back into the mill. I watched him go and then took a long, slow walk over Papa's meadow. It seemed funny to me to hear someone not a Friend talk so plain about God. Lots of folks talked about 'halleluias' and 'blessings', and 'The Will of God' as if they knew for certain just what it was, but then they didn't live no different from folks who didn't talk that way. Amongst the Friends, we talked that way on meeting days some, but generally our folks tried to live it too. That's why my Papa was dead or gone. I didn't know if I wanted to live like a Friend nor a Christian if it meant this kind of suffering. When I'd thought about this a while, Connor came out and offered to have his man drive me home on the wagon, which was to go back to Crabtree's place for more corn. So ended my first talk with Connor O'Keefe, my friend.

Over the next five days, I found one excuse after another to walk over to Crabtree's farm and sooner or later I found Connor. Sometimes he was out on patrol but like as not I'd find him doing some sort of work where he could talk about our families and the war. The rest of the Yankees, Sergeant Llewellyn and the others, were polite, but they didn't have no interest in talking to a little girl. But Connor always talked to me like I was a person. Once he even called me 'Mary' by accident, so in my mind I decided he was my big brother I never had. I cannot speak of how much comfort this was to me in those coldest days.

The 64th Virginia was gone clean out of the county; Major Beeres and the 16th Illinois drove them out of Hickory Flat, seven miles east of Jonesville, that first day. The world seemed to be taking on a new balance or beauty. Days were crisp and some snow fell on Cumberland Mountain. We got cold rain that froze and iced over the roads. The air nipped my nose and ears, but I didn't mind at all—there was something like a little flame in my heart again.

That is, until Sixth Day morning and I went to Crabtree's to find the Yankees packed and mounted, lining their horses up in columns by squad and company. I rushed amongst the horsemen searching desperately for Connor, nearly getting trampled. Finally, I found him riding on Willie next to Sergeant Llewellyn.

"Connor! Connor!" I cried, grabbing his boot. He looked down and smiled.

"Oh, I'm glad to see you before I go. You, take care now, girl." I couldn't think of anything to say. Maybe my face said it all. He looked troubled for a moment, reached around his neck and under the collar of his deep blue tunic, pulling out something shiny. He leaned down and put it in my hands. "This is to remember me, Maggie." Then he touched my cheek, "Don't lose faith, girl."

"Move out!" yelled a voice and he sat up looking around. Throwing me a last wink, he trotted off behind Sergeant Llewellyn and I was lost in the crunching of hundreds of hooves in the icy mud. I watched them go out the Crabtree lane and turn west towards the Gap. After a few minutes they were gone like they'd never been there.

I opened my hand. On a leather thong was a little silver cross with Jesus crucified on it. I was shocked. My Lord, Connor was a Catholic. I suppose if I'd known more of the world I would have guessed it right off, but I didn't know much more than what was in the Bible, George Fox's sermons and what Papa had told me. Catholics worshipped idols, like this little one, indulged in vanities like praying for the souls of the dead, and weren't Christian at all. They were in league with the Devil. Did I believe that? I don't know. I reckon Papa never saw a real Catholic in his life, never knew one. I did. I slipped the thong over my head and hid the crucifix in my dress, then ran home as fast as I could go.

My resolve to tell Miss Emily about Captain Garson was put to the test two days later. Mama and Mrs. Shelburn decided that all us children, except Baby John, who was still nursing, must stay at Grandfather's until Mrs. Shelburn's garden started growing. There just wasn't enough food left on the farm to feed us all and Grandma Mitchie had offered to help. We went down for meeting on First Day in Grandfather's wagon and afterwards, he took Mama and Mrs. Shelburn home. I was glad, for though William, Little Mary and Robert kept me busy, just a change of scenery thawed my cold heart a little.

Living in town again was a shock though. If people didn't care for Friends before, since the Yankees came through and stayed on the Crabtree farm, they hated us with us vengeance. There was no Josiah to shield me this time. About the only friend I had in town was Miss Emily. And to Miss Emily's I went, first chance I got. Grandma Mitchie let me go, but there was worry in her voice. I didn't pay it no mind at first but I thought about it afterwards.

It was two days until Christmas, that late afternoon that I went, but Jonesville wasn't putting up much of a show. It snowed lightly most of the day, though it didn't stick down in town, but turned into mud and ice. For those two days I overheard folks talk about men coming home on furlough, but nobody had been furloughed from the Confederate Army since the first year that anyone could remember, so it was just talk after all. If they weren't talking about furlough, they talked about the rumors just now leaking south about General Lee losing a big battle last summer up in Pennsylvania. With General Longstreet at loose ends down in east Tennessee and General Lee in retreat to the north and east, Virginia looked ripe for invasion. Christmas seemed mighty dreary, and the winter was the coldest in memory for lots of folks. I heard these things as I went to stores and ran errands for Grandma Mitchie. Usually, I heard them in snatches before men and women fell silent and glared at me, the traitor and Yankee-lover, the abolitionist's daughter, the deserter's daughter. A couple of days of this gave me a thicker skin. What did I care for what they thought? I had my friends.

Still, I remember a sense of something stuck in my throat that cold evening I crunched through the muddy ice up Jonesville's main street. I was grateful nobody was out. Windows were lit up and I prayed that people would be too busy to look out and see the Quaker girl going up the street. Miss Emily lived about as far out of town on the east side as Grandfather Andrew lived on the west, so it turned out to be a long walk. Snow started to fall again and I listened to it. I love the way snow eats sound, so that when it's snowing, you hear it because it's actually quieter than quiet. I stuck out my tongue and ate some. I started to thinking about this and other Christmases when I looked up to realize I stood in front of her house. I walked up the steps carefully, because they looked icy, and knocked on the big white door. My knock sounded hollow, like there was a big cave behind the door, and for just a second I imagined that I was Jane Eyre standing at the door of Thornfield Hall. No one answered for the longest time, so that I started to turn around and consider my path down through the ice on the steps when I heard the doorjamb smack and creak and the door swing open. There stood a Negro woman looking at me with quizzical eyes.

"What you want, child?"

"I come to see Miss Emily; she's my teacher."

"Well, she don't teach nobody no more. She said she don't want to see nobody." And the woman made a start at closing the door. The not-shy Maggie rose in me.

"But thee doesn't understand. I have news about Captain Garson!" The door was just about shut but it stopped at the sound of that name. Oh, the power of the name of one man. The woman stared at me, took at look back somewhere into the house and licked her lips.

"Awright. Come in here and wait. I'll go see if da mistress will see you." She let me into the dark hall and closed the door behind me. The entry hall was dark, even with a high window above the door. Paintings of grim, proud men in fine clothes and long wigs lined the wall on each side. They must have been the Tanner men down through the years, clear back to England. I thought then that each of them looked very unhappy, and if I were that unhappy, I wouldn't want my painting painted that way, much less hung up for everyone to see.

"Dis way, young lady," the woman said so that I jumped, surprised at her slipping in so silently. She led me into the parlor where a blazing fire sent leaping shadows across the walls. Miss Emily sat in the chair closest by the fire, dressed all in black, with an open book in her lap. But she wasn't reading. She stared into the fire, even when I came in. The door closed behind me. I stood and waited for her to say something in greeting, but she continued to look into the fire. The not-shy Maggie in me said, "Good evening Miss Emily."

"Good evening, Maggie," she replied so softly that I wasn't sure I'd heard her at first. I began to feel that everything was wrong and I wished I hadn't come. Could I still politely withdraw? I looked around the room for the door. This somehow stirred her to look at me.

"How could you?" she asked, anger and disbelief in her voice.

"Ma'am?" I said, though it wasn't what Friends were supposed to say.

"I hear tell you and yours helped out those Yankees that invaded our county. I know your folks don't believe in fighting, and I was willing to accept that on Christian principles, but to aid the enemy? And you seen there with them day after day. Don't you know they're our enemy? They're my enemy. How can you be friends with my enemy and be my friend?" She looked very provoked with me. So my visits to Crabtree farm had been talk here in town. Her question was a good question, one I'd been trying to shape since Caleb Pennington brought me the war. Who was my enemy anyway? But I couldn't concentrate on that right this moment. I felt tight in every muscle, guilty but not quite sure why, like when your folks punish you for something and you're not sure you did it. The not-shy Maggie was no help to me here. Anything that side of me might say seemed like impertinence, and I loved Miss Emily too much for that. She finally turned her glare away from me and back to the fire. "Well," she sighed, "I am told you have news about Jonathan. It would be a comfort to be sure of his resting place."

I spoke through desert dry lips and with a thick tongue, "He ain't dead, Miss Emily."

She turned to me quickly and her eyes flashed. "Tell me, quick, child."

"Well, I saw him and some other prisoners being marched to the Gap. He had bandages on the right side of his face and on his right arm, but he didn't look bad hurt. I'm sorry, Miss Emily."

She opened her mouth but didn't speak for a few seconds. "When was this?"

"Week ago yesterday. I came as soon as I could."

She turned back to the fire and I could see the shine of tear streaks down her face. "Oh, this is such...Oh, my poor Jonathan." She put her face in her hands and cried real hard. I could only guess what was going through her heart just then, expecting to be a widow before she was a bride, to find out that she might yet be a bride, and yet to know her man was in chains for no one knows how many years to come. I thought of my own Papa, probably dead. No wonder she couldn't say anything more.

I figured this was as good a time as any to leave. I said, "Goodbye, Miss Emily," but I don't think she heard me. I let myself out into the hall with the sad paintings and out the front door, down the icy steps. How could I be her friend and Connor's friend too? Did I have to choose? Did I have to take a firm side in this war? The questions rang through my head as snow began to fall thick like lace shaking out of the sky into the growing night.

IX
A Christmas Surprise

By Christmas Eve, a couple of days later, I had thoroughly made up my mind to regain Miss Emily's trust and regard. I decided my brief friendship with Connor O'Keefe was a poorly considered lapse and my father's desertion paid for by his death. Right or wrong, Lee County folks were my folks and there wasn't any getting away from that. I even took to practicing saying 'you' again in Grandfather's outbuildings. Of course, folks in town were no friendlier, but I'd show them I was really one of them. Miss Emily was right to put trust in me. I hardly thought more than that about my father; it was too complicated. Nor did I put off wearing Connor's crucifix. I didn't feel real clear about this resolve, but if I faltered, one thought of Miss Emily's tears was enough to bolster my resolve—that is until Christmas Eve.

That icy, sun washed morning before Christmas the sound of hundreds of hooves tapping and thundering outside Grandfather's door made me drop my cleaning and rush to the front parlor windows. The whole world was men in blue uniforms riding onto Grandfather's farm. Grandfather came out the front door and greeted Major Beeres like they were old friends. Then I saw Connor dismounting Willie in the front row, and all my loyalty to my country melted like snow in a thaw. I found myself running outside, but I stopped myself short of embarrassing myself and partially hid behind Grandfather. Maybe Connor wouldn't even notice me. Grownups sometimes are like that; they forget you if you're not part of their business. But Connor spotted me and smiled. He handed his reins to another soldier and came right up to us, shaking Grandfather's hand and reaching out to shake mine too. "How are you keeping, Maggie?" I hadn't lost my big brother at all.

Grandfather invited everyone in for refreshments and it became real clear to me that Grandma Mitchie didn't have enough of anything to feed and refresh the three-hundred or more Yankees in the battalion. But Major Beeres saw this right away and detailed a sergeant to bed the men in Grandfather's empty workers' cabins and their horses in the barn, and prepare their own Christmas celebrations. Then he and his three lieutenants, his three sergeants and Connor were invited in. Quick as thinking about it, Grandfather's farm became battalion headquarters for the next few days. So even if I had decided to earn Miss Emily's respect, I couldn't do anything but be associated with the Yankees.

But I didn't think long about that; our slow, uneventful, placid Quaker Christmas got turned into a Yankee Christmas right quick. Quakers don't really celebrate Christmas except maybe to eat a little more and work a little less. But suddenly our Christmas was full, with a tall decorated tree in Grandfather's parlor, shining with baubles and candles glowing like stars on its branches. Connor and the other Yankees sang "Deck the Halls", "Hark the Herald Angels Sing", and one real pretty one I'd never heard before but will never forget, "Silent Night." I think my heart broke when Sergeant Llewellyn finished that one. Nobody had any presents, but Major Beeres was gracious and told Grandfather that his hospitality was present enough for all his men. At this, the Yankees gave three cheers for Senator Milbourn. Grandfather blushed, something I'd never seen him do.

For me, the music was the perfect present and I never forgot it. I can't hear "Silent Night" without thinking of those happy faces singing like they was at home instead of in the middle of a war, and it always brings me to tears. I made a third resolve, that whatever else I did, I would never abandon music again. It was a high old time. Sergeant Llewellyn and Aunt Sarah got real sweet on each other. They sat next to each other, and the sergeant led each song in a sweet, strong, tenor voice that seemed like the singing of an angel in heaven. Sarah joined him in a high, clear soprano that none of us knew she had. Sarah got to calling him 'David' and he to calling her 'Sarah' and I could see Grandma Mitchie was fretted by it. But what could she do? Not much. Aunt Elizabeth had eyes for Lieutenant Foster, but he didn't pay her much mind. Yet Sarah wasn't hiding no feelings and David wasn't either. I figured Aunt Sarah would be read out of meeting sooner or later for marrying out of the faith. And Grandma Mitchie would love her just the same; I'd love her even more.

And I realized that much of what held me to my beliefs was sheer fear of Papa's anger. I think that night, if there was any Quaker left in me, it began to leak out—that is, except for one thing: I realized I could have no enemies. I loved Connor O'Keefe as I loved Emily Tanner. I realized it in the flash of a moment, unexpected, like lightning out of a clear sky, as we sang about the Christ child in the manger bringing the tidings of peace and good will to all men; all men, not just the Friends, or Yankees, but Catholics and Confederates and Methodists too. They were all loved by the Christ child, and so they were all my friends too. This thought took hold of me like a vision while we sang "Silent Night" and I knew it was True. I don't know how, but I had no doubts in my mind. Nor did I think of the price of the knowledge at that moment. I was in the starry heavens themselves as David Llewellyn's pure tenor voice soared over the little stable in Bethlehem. And I was at peace for the first time like I never was before. I knew what I believed and it was a great comfort to me. Only later was I to discover the full price of the Truth.

I saw that Papa had paid the price of his life for the Truth I now believed. And I began to understand his quiet side more, the side that I always thought veiled his anger, now it was plain as day that his peace with the Truth left him few words to say and that his anger was short lived. I ached to tell him again, but as each day had passed, my hope that he might still be alive faded. Connor shook his head sadly when I asked him if he'd found out about Papa. The fire died and Yankees fell asleep on the carpet where they lay around the tree and David Llewellyn whispered to Aunt Sarah. Grandma Mitchie led the officers up to guest bedrooms. I got up to leave when Aunt Elizabeth did. I paused a second, and in my peace, I kissed Connor on the forehead and followed Aunt Elizabeth upstairs to the attic bedroom where William, Robert and little Mary had long since gone to sleep, carried to their beds by Grandfather with the wonder of the glistening tree in their dreams. When I looked downstairs I just saw David Llewellyn kiss Aunt Sarah in the shadows in the hall at the foot of the stairs. That made me really happy.

Yet that Christmas Eve the wind blew fiercely and it got colder in Jonesville than I can possibly remember. The shutters rattled so that I forgot my happiness. I hardly slept, for the wind sounded like the moaning of dead soldiers, Yankee and Confederate both. I dreamed fitfully of the whole of

Grandma's house being filled with bloody soldiers crying for water in the dim light with curtains drifting in the unfelt wind. I woke up shivering and didn't sleep again.

Christmas day was anything but quiet, at least not quiet the way Quaker Christmases had been before. Grandfather gave our front sitting room over to Major Beeres, who turned it into battalion headquarters. Yankees were stomping in and out at all hours, taking papers and leaving papers and saluting. By night, Lieutenants Alger, Reece, Foster, and Major Beeres shared the two remaining guest bedrooms. Connor and the sergeants shared the parlor floor by the fire. The house was full up.

I wouldn't have been surprised to find them all gone the day after Christmas, but Connor told me they were here for a while. So I felt resigned to life as a Yankee collaborator and all the grief I'd get for it next time Grandma Mitchie sent me into town. You can imagine my surprise then, the day after Christmas when Grandma Mitchie sent me down to the far corn crib, and I opened the door to find myself looking down the black barrel of a revolver nearly as long as my arm.

I clapped my hand over my mouth to keep from screaming. For a long time all I heard was my own breathing and my faint heartbeat. A voice from the dark whispered, "Close the door, girl!" Naturally, I obeyed. I knew that voice. As my eyes got used to the little light that leaked in through the air slits between the side slats, I slowly made out the face. My Lord, it was Captain Garson! His coat was torn and bloody around the right arm and there was still a bandage around his head. He let the hammer down slowly and lowered the pistol, whispering harsh words just under his breath. "Well, I ain't going to shoot no child. So what are you going to do now, Miss Milbourn? Turn me in, I reckon." He leaned his head back and closed his eyes in despair and exhaustion. He let the pistol sag in front of me.

It was a good question. What was I going to do? I don't recall pausing one second once that pistol was down. I grabbed it and much to my own surprise, came up with it and pointed it straight at Captain Garson. He opened his eyes and froze.

"Did thee hang my Papa?" I demanded. My blood was on fire. I felt determined that if he did I would shoot him—maybe. Even as I tried to steel my resolve, the image of the Babe in the manger came before my mind.

"No, miss. We never caught him, though you were lying through your teeth that day at your house, I'll be bound."

The not-shy, not-Quaker Maggie answered, "Wouldn't you?" He didn't answer, so I figured it was my turn to question. "How'd you get here, right in the middle of all these Yankees too?"

"I was coming up through town day before yesterday and the whole pack of them come riding in. I hid in the nearest corn crib. Should've known they'd all light at your grandfather's farm, but I wasn't thinking straight. Hadn't eaten since I took a pistol and run from the guard at Ball's bridge." Then he shivered and pulled his coat tighter around him with his good left arm.

Then I knew just what I was going to do. I stuffed the pistol into the bottom of the basket I'd brought for corn and then loaded it up with as many cobs as it could hold, talking all the while. "This is what we're going to do, Captain. You're going to wait here. I'm going back into town and fetch Miss Emily. Between us, we'll figure a way to get you out of here."

His eyes squinted with distrust. "I thought you were all cozy with the Yanks. Why should I believe you?"

"Well, Captain, one, you ain't got no choice, and two, if I wanted to turn you in, I could've done it before now." That was the way Uncle Joel used to talk when he gave me reasons to do what he said. It worked real well with Captain Garson. He shut right up and leaned back.

"Ain't you going to give me back my pistol, with all these Yankees about?"

"No. They ain't going to find you, and I don't want you to shoot any of them in the meanwhile. Ain't nobody comes in here but me."

He grimaced, "I'll be waiting."

"I'll be back," I replied, slipping out through the door and latching it on the outside. I went straight to Grandma Mitchie in the kitchen and unloaded the corn, being careful to let the cloth in the basket cover the pistol. Then I took it upstairs as if I'd forgotten to drop it in the kitchen. When I got to my room that I shared with the other children, (they were all out playing) I hid it up in the back of the top drawer of the dresser, where even William was too short to find it. Then I rushed the basket downstairs and pleaded with Grandma Mitchie, "Please, can I go see Miss Emily this morning?"

"Has thee done all thy chores?"

I knew I hadn't but I wanted everything natural. "No, but when I was getting the corn I thought about how Miss Emily has so little and is near going hungry. Couldn't we give her a load of corn?" It was probably true. Nearly everyone in town was running short, though frugal farmers like Grandfather were better off than most.

"Well, that's thoughtful of thee, Maggie. Yes," she said, pausing to think, "help thy Aunt Elizabeth haul the laundry out and then thee can go."

I can tell you that laundry never went out so fast in the history of that house. Before you could wink, I was hopping down the main street of Jonesville, skirting the ice and singing "Silent Night" softly to myself. The wind was fierce cold. It seemed like the coldest winter I could remember. Clouds were building up over Cumberland Mountain.

Suddenly, the sound of hooves clattered around me and I looked up to see Connor riding on Willie with a patrol behind him. My first feeling was guilt, especially when he asked me, "Where are you headed, Maggie?"

Oh Lord, if it could have been anybody else. Well, I wasn't going to lie to him. Was I betraying my big brother? No, it'd be no skin off his nose if they didn't catch Captain Garson. Why, they'd lost him already. The not-shy Maggie looked my friend in the face with a clean conscience and a full heart. "Well, I'm going to visit my teacher. She don't like Yankees none, but she's a good teacher."

"I reckon she is," Connor replied, smiling, and bidding me farewell, he and the patrol trotted on. I almost ran to Miss Emily's house after that. When I knocked on the door it took even longer for the Negro lady to answer this time. When she did, her creased eyebrows and slight frown told me that I was the last person she expected to see again.

"What's you want, child?"

"I must see Miss Emily. It's urgent."

She stood there for a minute, thinking about this. I didn't want to use Captain Garson's name again; Miss Emily might not want this woman to know. I prayed to the Lord Jesus to move this woman's heart. It must have worked, because the next second she let me in saying, "I don' know, child. I'll go see if Miss Emily will see you." I waited in the hall with the paintings of the men with long, sour faces. It seemed to me that this war was the doing of men with long faces and longer pride. The handle turned and clicked on the parlor door, and the woman opened it. I walked in to find Miss Emily seated by the fire much as before. She glared at me, but I wasn't surprised.

"Well," she said real short and offended, "I see your family is determined to collaborate with the enemy. I can hardly think this is a social visit. What have you come to tell me?"

"I've got Captain Garson. I need your help to get him out." Lord, her eyes got big and her face changed in an instant. "Oh, my dear child," and she caressed my face in her hands. I loved it. I loved her. "But why are you telling me this, with Yankees all over the place?" Well, I think the shy Maggie in me was dead and gone.

"He ain't my enemy, Miss Emily." It was truthful, but hardly a full explanation. But how could I tell her what I discovered Christmas Eve? I could barely understand it myself, much less put it in words. She looked at me bewildered, but I figured we didn't have any time. "You got to get your wagon and come over to the farm."

"With all them Yankees?"

I didn't answer, but I could see her steel herself. She knew he'd be spotted walking for sure. It had to be the wagon. I went on. "Grandma Mitchie said I could give you some corn. Captain Garson's hiding in the back corn crib. You got to bring a big blanket too. If anyone asks you, it's to keep the corn dry." I didn't do a very good job of explaining it, but I think she got the idea. She called to her woman, "Martha!"

The Negro woman opened the door, "Yes, Miss?"

"Have John hitch the wagon. I'm driving myself."

"Yes, Miss."

She went out for a moment, returning with a heavy cloak. We mounted up in Miss Emily's yard and clattered off through the icy mud on the street. I found inside me for the first time I could remember, no voices at all of guilt or unease. I was acting on my beliefs and the simplicity of it made me just feel like I was glad to be alive and there wasn't anything else to be said. I wish, even now, that I could feel like that more often.

In a few minutes we came onto Grandfather's farm and the sentries passed us by with a wave when they saw me. I could see Miss Emily stiffen at the sight of all the Yankees swarming around us like bees around a hive. I put my hand on hers.

"Go that way, Miss Emily," I pointed to the lane that went up to the back corn cribs. At the fourth crib, we stopped and I got down to open the door. Suddenly, a voice startled me.

"What are you doing, Miss?"

Well, maybe I wasn't the shy Maggie anymore, but I found out right then that I was sure ready to be scared. Lieutenant Foster sat up on a big white horse with an unhappy look on his face. I suddenly felt very glad that Captain Garson hadn't any pistol. I tried to collect myself and answered, "What Grandma told me." Lieutenant Foster looked irritated. "No, what are you doing with that corn and this woman?"

"She's is our neighbor. We're sharing."

"That corn is for the battalion."

Nobody had said anything to Grandfather about needing his corn. The Yankees pretty much had all they could get from the farms down Long Hollow. I felt myself get real angry, that warlike feeling. Connor told me once that Lieutenant Foster thought too much of himself. So I depended on it. "Well," I said, "Let's just go see what Major Beeres has to say about that." Lieutenant Foster didn't flinch. Things couldn't get worse, but they did.

"What's that?" my grandfather's voice interrupted, and there he was standing at the head of Miss Emily's horse in his dirty work shirt and flat brimmed black hat. My heart sank. I couldn't say what he'd do.

I answered up, "Grandma says I can give some corn to my teacher, Miss Emily, and the Lieutenant here says it's for the army."

Grandfather smiled pleasantly at Miss Emily and said, "Good morning, Sister Emily." She had looked whiter than new snow on the ground since the Yankee lieutenant came up, but Grandfather's greeting restored her some. Grandfather looked up at Lieutenant Foster and said, "Thy commander has not asked me for my corn, brother. Will he soon?"

The lieutenant looked a little embarrassed at being caught out, his lips tight shut like he didn't dare say what he wanted to say. I could see that Grandfather had gauged his mettle right away, and trapped him neatly between overstepping his authority and answering at all. "I will have to go consult the Major," he said crisply and walked his horse off up to the house. We only had a few seconds now with no Yankees around, but Grandfather said to Miss Emily, "Let me help thee load thy wagon." What could I do?

There was no way to get rid of him. And before I could speak, he'd ducked into the corn crib. I swallowed hard and ducked in after him.

It was just what I feared. There Grandfather stood facing Captain Garson, the man who'd chased his three sons out of the country, capturing two of them and impoverishing one of them. There Grandfather looked on a man fighting to defend slavery and separate his state from his country. Grandfather, stooped over there in the dimness of the crib looked at Captain Garson for endless seconds then back over his shoulder at me. What could I say to him? It would have to be the truth. Words came out of my mouth.

"I have no enemies, Grandfather." If my soul depended on it, I could not guess what he would do next. He nodded and whispered to me, "Thy conscience is thy guide." Without another word, he extended his left hand to Captain Garson and helped him to stand stooped, saying, "Go quickly, soldier. Thy adversaries have left for the time being." Captain Garson looked bewildered at Grandfather for only a second then limped out of the crib. While Emily made him lie down in the bed of the wagon and covered him with the blanket, Grandfather and I filled four baskets with ears of corn and piled them over the blanket so that it looked like a pile of corn. The instant we'd done so, Emily leapt to the seat of the wagon and took up the reins. For a moment she turned to us and said, "God bless you."

I couldn't speak from my wrung heart. Grandfather replied, "God bless thee, sister."

She slapped the reins and rode off the farm right past the sentries and off into Jonesville. Grandfather put his hand around my shoulder. "Thee is a brave girl and a true Christian, child. Well then, isn't it about time for dinner?" I wiped my eyes and nodded. Somehow, when I gave up being Quaker it seemed I became more Quaker than ever. I didn't understand it at all. He led me in for the midday meal.

X

The Storm Breaks

I think that I supposed the time of danger over. Life fell into a routine with Yankees all around the place. Lieutenant Foster never mentioned the corn again, nor did he look me in the eye. The week passed and I made no attempt to see Miss Emily. I felt as if I had somehow left that part of my life somewhere in the past. On the eve of Fifth Day, many of the Yankees got drunk and whooped around great bonfires to well past midnight in the frosty air. Major Beeres and his officers stayed up till Grandma's clock struck midnight and toasted each other with wine in their mess cups. Grandma didn't own any wine glasses to offer them. They toasted President Lincoln, Colonel Lemert, General Wilcox, General Grant, the Union and victory in 1864. I saw it all sitting in the cold and darkness on the stairs long after Grandma sent me to bed. Thus, I witnessed my first New Year's Eve as a past Quaker.

Most of the Yankees were sick the next day, but things seemed normal enough by Seventh Day, except that it just kept getting colder. It got down to freezing well before sunset. It was as if the warmth of men's hatred for each other was answered by the absolute cold of the weather. I went to bed Seventh Day evening expecting to sit through another meeting next morning.

I woke with a start to the sound of distant gunfire, that sound like rocks thrown against the barn, cracking and ripping. I sat up. My brothers and sisters still slept. Outside first light had just coming creeping in from the east. A clear shell of ice encased the branches outside the window, which shivered in the wind. Who would fight or even go outside on such a day? Thick clouds darkened half the sky so that one moment it was sunny and the next stormy. At first I couldn't find the will to move. Then I couldn't get to the window fast enough. My window faced east, toward the center of Jonesville and nothing was to be seen in that direction. But the popping grew louder and I felt like screaming with the tension gripping my heart. I threw on my dress, not bothering to fix my hair into a bun, nor get my bonnet, and raced downstairs so recklessly I almost fell and rolled down the steps.

Grandfather, Grandma Mitchie, Elizabeth, and Sarah stood in the sitting room where the windows faced the west road out to Long Hollow. The major and all the other Yankees had vanished, leaving papers strewn all over the major's desk. I wedged myself in between Grandfather and Grandma Mitchie to see and hear. The popping sounded louder on this side of the house and Yankee soldiers were running from Grandfather's land up the road, carrying their rifles, some of them still pulling on their pants and boots.

"Grandfather," I asked, swallowing so I could talk, "Are they headed this way?"

He didn't answer for some time, then finally said, "Maggie, get thy brothers and sister and get down to the cellar and stay there."

I figured that for a 'yes' and bolted upstairs to get William, Little Mary and Robert downstairs. They still slept and Mary and Robert woke crying for the suddenness of my waking them. I held Mary and commanded the puzzled William, "Thee must play the man today. Soldiers are fighting near here and we must get to the cellar this instant. Get Robert." William, without so much as a twitch in his face, rose and pulled Robert out of the room and down the stairs. He was Papa's son all right. I got Little Mary down the stairs behind while she cried for Mama. Just as we hit the first floor I heard the windows in the sitting room and the kitchen shatter. Grandfather cried out, "Get down on the floor!" from in the sitting room. William had frozen for a moment, but I shoved him to the cellar door and followed him down. It was mighty dark down there and it took me a while to find the candle by the door and light it. Once it flickered I saw that it was less than half a candle; I would have to go out and find at least one more. I got William, Robert and Mary to huddle together in the warmest corner of the cellar, but I saw right away it would not be enough. They needed blankets if they were going to stay down here. I went up the cellar stairs cautiously. The firing still popped outside. I made a dash for the kitchen, seeing no one in the sitting room—no bodies either—Grandfather had gotten everybody safely out of the way. When I reached the kitchen I could see that all the south side windows had been shot out. Just near my head in the wall I heard a sharp slapping sound and saw out of the corner of my eye the round hole form itself just the same instant. I dropped down to the floor and crawled across to the cupboard with the candles. I don't recall being afraid—my heart pumped too fast. It felt more like when you're running as hard as you can and some force comes in you that gives you more strength than you thought you had.

With my fistful of candles I crawled out of the kitchen and dashed up the stairs to our room, wrenching the blankets off our beds and dashing back down the stairs. I met Grandma Mitchie half way down. Her eyes looked more frightened than I'd ever seen them.

"What is thee doing, child?"

I couldn't find words in my excited state, but she must have figured it out without my answer. "Get thee down below, quick, Maggie," she commanded and I did. I almost slid down the cellar stairs, but not before another couple of bullets slapped into the wall in the entry hall. William, Mary, and Robert huddled in the near dark, their candle guttering and almost out, fear in their eyes. The not-shy, strong Maggie in me rose. I found words. "Don't thee worry. We're safe down here and it won't last too long." Lies. Lies. Lies, I found.

Through the open cellar door I heard the slapping sound of bullets hitting the house. At first it happened every minute or so, then it started to happen faster and faster, like rain when it starts as a sprinkle and slowly builds up to being a downpour. We heard the thump of a cannon going off seven or ten times. Then there was the sound of many boots clomping through the entry hall. Looking up the cellar stairs I saw Yankees rushing in Grandfather's house, up the main stairs and toward each room. "Oh, my Lord. The fight's coming here." Then I wished I hadn't spoken, because Robert and Mary really started to cry hard. I held them closer.

I reckon I would have spent the battle that way if I hadn't looked up and seen Yankees carrying in wounded men on planks and stretchers. After four or five went by I clearly saw the unconscious face of the sixth one; it was Connor.

I reckon it was pretty foolish, but I handed William the candle and rushed up the cellar stairs like I was crazy. Teams of Yankees bearing stretchers wound up stairs like a long blue caterpillar. I broke into the line and fought my way upstairs around the stretcher bearers. They kept going up into the attic, some of them coming down now dangling the empty stretchers at their sides as they squeezed past the bearers going up. The house absolutely crackled with the patter of bullets hitting the sides, like sparks crackling in a fire when you shift a log over. I didn't care. Let them take me, I had to find out.

I found Connor down toward the end of the line. Blood oozed all over the floor, but I made myself not see any of it. That was the not-shy Maggie who had taken me completely over. The rest of me lay dead somewhere, just as some of these blue soldiers did. And so I looked on death the first time and knew that I could bear it. I could stand up to it in all its hideous unnatural ugliness.

When I came to Connor, I took his hand. "Connor? I'm here. It's me, Maggie."

He rolled his head over and opened his eyes a little. When he spoke his voice sounded hoarse and his lips dry. "Maggie. Good of you to come. Sorry I can't get up." He closed his eyes and leaned his head back, his lips smacking of dryness as he barely opened his mouth. "I'm done for."

My heart plunged down. "No! You can make it. You've got to make it."

He shook his head. "No. I'm gut shot. Just a matter of time."

He reached a hand into his uniform and I thought for a second he meant to show me his wound where the blood puddled near the bottom of his left ribs. But he reached higher and pulled out a photograph and two letters and handed all of that to me. "Fiona," he whispered, pausing to breathe between each utterance. "Mary. Mother. Father. Got to know."

The picture showed a beautiful girl in a fine dress standing under a parasol. With a little imagination I could almost picture her red hair and white skin though the photograph, of course, was brown.

"Promise?" he whispered.

I squeezed his hand. "Promise. Yes, I promise."

He let out a long breath and for a panicky moment, I thought I'd lost him, until he said, "Mary?"

I didn't know how to answer him, but he called the name several times, so finally I answered, "Yes, I'm here, Connor."

"Don't fuss about this, Mary. God's will. Understand?"

"Yes," I answered.

Then for a long time he breathed in and out with his eyes looking half open out the window. And then he just stopped and the pressure of his hand in mine went gradually limp. It happened so fast. Though the battle roared all around us, I knelt there in a pocket of absolute silence. I don't know how long that silence lasted, but finally I reached up and closed his eyes.

The silence stopped with the roar of the battle upon me. The walls pattered with bullets. Almost fifty men filled the attic, wounded or dead, laying in rough rows. Grandma Mitchie and Elizabeth rushed among them with water and towels while a Yankee surgeon went from man to man, muttering and shaking his head. Sarah knelt over one of the men in the far corner. Grandma saw me when I stood up and rushed over.

"Get thee down the cellar, Maggie!"

"No, Grandma." I surprised myself with the firmness of my voice. But I knew my own mind and conscience. "I want to help."

"Child, it is too dangerous."

"I want to help, Grandma."

She paused a moment, and I think she realized that I did not speak as a child.

"Well, help me, then." And I did, passing among the moaning men and the blood that stained the floor, Elizabeth and I brought towels, water and comfort to those for whom we could do little more. To some I read from scripture, and this was a comfort to them. Some merely wanted their hand held for a time. The hem of my dress became crimson against the plain grey cloth from kneeling in the pooled blood. I think my heart turned crimson too.

Oh, how many, many hours did it last? I couldn't tell. I was nearly sick more than once. Yet never did the bloody horror overwhelm me. I forgot myself and only looked into their needy eyes. I was strong for them. So that long, deadly day trudged on for what felt like a whole winter, and a spring, and a summer, fall, winter, then a year, then years and tens of years till the clouds darkened the sky.

Over the din of battle I heard a bugle sound and like a spell had been cast, our surgeon vanished, and the Yankees in our house streamed out, mounting their horses under fire, and rode north toward the back road to Cumberland Gap. I sent a prayer up that they would make it. As I did it, I realized the

Confederates would come soon and those still living would be prisoners. The thought made me sadder than anything I had yet seen. But at least the Confederates would have a surgeon.

About this time I made my way over to Aunt Sarah, to see the soldier she'd spent so much time on. And right away I knew why. David Llewellyn lay with a bloody bandage wrapped around his head, singing "Silent Night" deliriously. Sarah held his hand and tried to talk to him. My heart spoke before my head had time to fear. "Sarah, we've got to hide him. The Confederates are coming." She looked at me stricken. My mind raced until I remembered the little alcove in the room my brothers and sisters and I shared. I found an abandoned stretcher against the wall and brought it over to where David lay. Sarah stared at him in pain and shock. I grabbed her by the shoulders.

"Aunt Sarah, listen to me. We've got to hide David. The Confederates are coming. There's a place in my room if thee can help me carry him. Can thee do that, Auntie?"

Sarah stared dully for a while, like she didn't believe the words came out of my mouth.

"Come on!" I urged, shoving a stretcher next to David and I started gently lifting his head and shoulders onto it. Sarah suddenly came alive and got his feet and hips on it. Then we hustled David downstairs one flight. I say hustled, but it was hard work not falling on the stairs and pitching the poor man the rest of the way. He wasn't light. But at last we packed him into the large walk-in closet in the room Grandfather gave us children. I think Grandma once used it for storage, so the closet was half as big as the room. We lay David in there and covered him with clothes and blankets, and not a moment too soon. The lull in the fighting that had fallen not long after the Yankees made their escape, broke with the sound of orders shouted and clomping boots downstairs.

"Search the house!" I heard some soldier yell and a chill ran down my spine. David wouldn't stay hidden in a closet very long if they searched the way they did for Papa. Sarah and I spent some minutes listening to every bump and footstep below in helpless terror. But I couldn't stay that way long; my anger rose in me and I crept out to my dresser. There, under the petticoats in the top drawer, lay Captain Garson's horse pistol, cold, heavy and grey.

I took it out and crept back into the closet, firmly resolved to shoot any grey uniform that dared to come in. Sarah's eyes only got bigger with terror and I thought of that child in the manger, and my other resolve to have no enemies. But I just didn't see any way out of this one, so I prayed and just threw the whole thing into the manger for the child to have. I know that sounds odd, but it seemed the thing to do.

The clomping of boots drew nearer and sweat trickled down the side of my face. I heard my room door thrown open and crash against the wall. Then long silence. I cocked back the hammer on the pistol and aimed at the opening, wondering if I could really pull the trigger and blow a child of God to heaven or hell. I tried to steel my resolve by remembering how they'd killed Connor, but I couldn't work up the hatred somehow. I heard some furniture shoved around and some toys crash to the floor. Sarah trembled in absolute terror. Then the bootsteps moved to just outside the closet door. The first thing I saw was the big black boot come in, followed by another and then the uniform of a Confederate officer. The man froze on seeing my pistol pointed at his chest and only after a minute did I realize that I was pointing Captain Garson's pistol at Captain Garson himself.

"Well, Miss Maggie," he said, "You going to use that thing?"

Lord give me wisdom. "Well," I replied, "I reckon it depends on what you're going to do."

"What do you mean?" he asked. I didn't really know, and then suddenly it all made sense and I did know.

"Well, this Yankee is sort of a friend of the family and I don't want to see him no prisoner, 'specially as he ain't feeling so well. You should know, Captain, that being a prisoner ain't so good."

His eyes, which had squinted with curiosity till now, grew big. I kept talking without a thought—the words just ran out of me like water through a hole in a barrel.

"I guess I expect that those who have been shown mercy should show some mercy themselves."

He looked perplexed for only a moment and then I could see by his eyes that he understood the exchange I proposed. But would he buy it? His duty to his country might not allow him. It would be easy for him to say so, then come back with more soldiers and take David with a show of force. In the wrinkles on his brow, I could see the debate taking place in his mind. And somewhere from within me I understood what I must do next. I let the hammer down gently on the pistol, turned the handle toward him and held it up, saying, "I think this is yours, Captain." Well, that absolutely floored him. It took him some seconds before he had the presence of mind to take the pistol from me. Then, suddenly a voice shouted from the landing, "You all right, Captain?"

Captain Garson stood speechless, holding two pistols and a whole lot else in his hands.

"Captain?" Bootsteps came into the room.

Captain Garson stood up straight and turned around. "Nothing here, sergeant. Take your detail downstairs and get those Yankee wounded to the surgeon. Then get started on graves."

"Where Captain?"

I thought of Connor. I wanted him buried on Grandfather's farm. He was my brother. I made a downward pointing gesture and Captain Garson caught it out of the side of his eye.

"Here, sergeant. On this man's land. He harbored 'em alive, he can keep 'em dead. And tell Colonel Pridemore I'll be along in a minute. Go on, now."

The bootsteps cleared out of the room. Captain Garson looked at me wordlessly for a minute, nodded farewell and disappeared. Sarah and I sat through the twilight, the darkness and long hours into the night, waiting with shallow breath for the pounding of boots up the stairs, waiting for treachery. When I heard Grandfather's clock strike midnight I knew it was true. They would never come. The Captain was a man of honor. I got up to search for the rest of the family.

XI
Long Roads and Returns

They buried Connor and the others in front of Grandfather's house. I stood there by the trench, fingering the crucifix under my dress and trying to say prayers. Grandfather stood by me, silent, with his arm around my shoulder. I had no tears then—I spent them all in the attic. I had some letters to write.

Two days later, Sarah drove a wagonload of corn west, toward my Papa's farm, with me on board. We drove right past the Confederate soldiers who occupied the town the rest of that winter. No one tried to stop us. When we reached my home, Mama was overjoyed to see me alive and to hear we'd all survived. But we didn't stop very long. By nightfall we made the Cumberland Gap and unburied David from under the corn. There we told Colonel Lemert the sad story of how Major Beeres and the 16th Illinois had surrendered to five Confederate regiments that had them surrounded, and how they'd escaped Grandfather's house and made a stand till they ran out of bullets. Then Sarah gave me a hug and a kiss and David squeezed my hands weakly. Sarah went on with my letters to Connor's family, and to become the bride of David Llewellyn, read out of meeting just like I always thought. I took the wagon on alone and rode back to Grandfather's.

About this time I found *Jane Eyre* stuffed in a corner of my room under an old apron. I finally accepted that Rochester was wounded. I had to. I too had lost some of myself and I felt Jane's wisdom to accept this in her man.

When spring finally came, General Jones and the five Confederate regiments rode out of town and Jonesville grew quiet again. Grandma Mitchie did what she could to restore the house, though a cannonball lodged forever in the porch and the bloodstains never did come off the attic floor.

Mrs. Shelburn's garden began to thrive and my brothers, sister and I came home. Lee County stayed quiet, except for a few months the following year when General Morgan's raiders stayed in Jonesville between raids on Ohio. Some Yankees chased a few of them out of town and things got quiet again. Then in April we heard that General Lee had surrendered a couple of days ride east at Appomattox Courthouse. General Johnston surrendered a few days later and the boys, those left, started coming home. Captain Garson become just Mr. Jonathon Garson, married Emily and moved into the Tanner house where I became a welcome and frequent guest. And he never again mentioned the Yankee prisoner he'd left to me. People in the town and down Long Hollow came to speak kindly to me again and I couldn't help but wonder if the Garsons had told my part in his escape.

Also at that time I learned that Josiah Clark died in the trenches surrounding Petersburg. I mourned for him deeply and long, as I did for Connor, resting outside Grandfather's door. For a time, my life seemed as bare as an elm in winter. But I had my family. Mrs. Shelburn left us in the fall when a good corn crop came in. She took her share and returned with our love to restart her own farm.

A year after the war ended I was at the newly rebuilt log school with the other children of Long Hollow, waiting for the new teacher to show up, watching the small children play in the yard when five men came walking down the road. Their clothes were torn and ragged and their long beards dirty. They carried very little. We were used to seeing forlorn soldiers returning home like tramps, so I thought nothing of it, even when Caleb Pennington chirped, "That's your Papa, Maggie."

"No, it ain't."

"Yes, it is. I swear."

I didn't believe him. If Papa was coming he would have written. But the men stopped and looked at us. One tall man came right up to me and I got scared until I saw his eyes. Papa's eyes. "Maggie?" he said, "My, girl, thee has grown some."

"Papa!" I cried and fell into his arms. Later when we got home and he sat shaved and in clean clothes, he squinted at me and said, "They tell me that thee has been brave, Maggie."

"It weren't nothing, Papa," I replied in typical family modesty. I didn't really mean it. I was not that girl three years before whom Caleb Pennington pelted with mud clods and I well knew it. I'd like to say that Papa and I always got along after this, but that isn't true. He was still the stubbornest man in Lee County, but I knew that he loved me, even when at age sixteen I hurt him by announcing to the family that I would begin attending the Methodist church. I don't recall why I chose that time to do it; by that age I saw myself like Jane Eyre, old enough to choose for herself no matter what any man might say.

Papa hung on in Lee County until I approached my twentieth birthday, though most folks hated him and his mill business died. He said he wanted to move west because he said there were no Friends for me to marry in Lee County, but I think that the neighbors finally wore down the rock of his heart. Or maybe it was the death of little Mary to scarlet fever two years after the war that cracked his heart a little. Maybe it was both. Lord knows I would never marry a Friend anyway and freely told him so. He pretended not to hear. We bought a big wagon, packed it with everything we could carry and all my brothers and sisters, including the three new brothers and a new sister, and kissed Grandfather, Grandma Mitchie and Uncle Joel goodbye. Then we gathered up the Crabtrees and the Bushes and their wagons and headed west across Kentucky, Illinois and Missouri, stopping long enough to visit Sarah and David and their children. Papa was wagon master, of course. We caught the railroad in Missouri and took it to the end of the line in Butler County, Kansas, where Papa homesteaded the land.

In spite of his talk, Papa, true to form, moved far from any meeting. I would not marry a Friend, though there weren't many to marry anyway. Nor would I marry just any old ignorant farmer. I taught school for some years and attended the Methodist church. It was some years before I met my Charles, an educated man and a good Methodist.

I still think of these things in quiet, sad moments, especially on winter days when the ice freezes on the branches like it did on the day of the battle in Jonesville. I think of Josiah and Connor and of Papa, and of the beauty of our home in Long Hollow, knowing that I never will return. But memories grow dim, like the last pages of a book read long ago. My girls, Ethel and Lucy, and my boy, Hiram, sit by me and listen on a winter's night. As I see their eyes glowing with the pleasure of the story in the firelight, I know that each of their lives is a book being written afresh.

Author's Note

Maggie Milbourn did live through the Civil War in Long Hollow. Though some of the characters are fictional, Maggie and all the family members were real live people, and I have tried to portray them as accurately as possible given little information. The fence jumping, the destruction of the school, the Union wounded in the attic at Grandfather Milbourn's place, and Joel Milbourn's escape from the conscriptors all actually happened. Henry and other Quakers being left for dead and escaping, Mrs. Shelburn and her garden, Old Pet carrying Henry to the Gap, and Mary Milbourn ripping off the barn doors to fool the conscriptors all actually happened. These are contained in the family record passed on from "Maggie" Margaret Canfield to her daughter Lucille Zulema Prothero, my grandmother. All the fighting I've portrayed as accurately as possible from Union and Confederate dispatches in the historical record.

amazon.com.

Amazon.com
1850 Mercer Rd.
Lexington, KY 40511

Gary W. Kroeker
Schurzelter Str. 548
52074 Aachen
Deutschland

Billing Address:
Gary W. Kroeker
Schurzelter Str. 548
52074 Aachen
Deutschland

DQDw2dRDR/-1 of 1-/std-intl-us-eur/4021713 1S

Your order of November 9, 2008 (Order ID 002-0412108-5333055)

Qty.	Item
	IN THIS SHIPMENT
1	**Maggie of Long Hollow** Prothero, James W. --- Paperback **(** P-1-B2C161 **) 1606729004** **1606729004**

Subtotal
Shipping & Handlin
Order Total
Paid via Mastercard
Balance due

This shipment completes your order.

151/DQDw2dRDR/-1 of 1-//1S/std-intl-us-eur/4021713/1110-14:30/1109-11:50/tott Pack Type: A

Shipping Address:
Gary W. Kroeker
Schurzelter Str. 548
52074 Aachen
Deutschland

Item Price	Total
$15.25	$15.25

	$15.25
ɜ	$7.98
	$23.23
	$23.23
	$0.00

Printed in the United States
128370LV00004B/142/P

9 781606 729007